CHANCE STRIKER

ONE IN A MILLION

WRITTEN BY SALWA EMERSON & BRIAN SALIBA
ILLUSTRATED BY NEIL KOHNEY

To Josiah—
Enjoy!

To NOBLE, BERLYN, and VANNER,
my mischievous muses!

And to ELVIS and SHERRY,
my faithful crossing guards at all of this year's forks in the road.
Thanks for always keeping watch over me.

—S.E.

To ZACK,
who always liked my stories.

—B.S.

© 2019 by Emerson Ink LLC

www.chancestriker.com

ISBN 978-1-7323603-0-3

Cover and Interior Design by Teresa Bonaddio

Printed in the United States of America

PROLOGUE

THE SCORE'S 2-2, and penalty kicks are tied 3-3.
If I can get this ball into the back of that net—and
past David de Gea, first—the US will have its first-
ever World Cup win. It all comes down to me and my
right foot.

The crowd's chanting, "Striker! Striker! Striker!"
as I walk to the penalty box. But once I reach
down and touch the ball, everything goes quiet.
The 100,000 people in Camp Nou, the three billion
people watching on TV, the cameras, the lights . . .
It all fades into the background. It's just me, rookie
star forward of the men's US soccer team, the ball,

the goal, and the best goalkeeper on the planet.

"Hold up," you may be thinking. "What are the chances that some kid named Striker ends up becoming a soccer player? And what are the chances he actually becomes a soccer star? And, seriously, what are the chances that this kid—a 12-year-old, no less!—can possibly win the World Cup? Like one a million?"

Here's the thing. I'm all about long odds. That's my name! Well, not exactly. My mom didn't actually name me Long Odds Striker. But she did name me Chance, and I am all about soccer, so I guess that answers your first question.

But if you're asking about the rest of it, well, remember, it's my dream after all!

So here I am, seconds away from being either the most popular kid on the planet or the kid who blew the US's first-ever World Cup title. I'd have to go into hiding, maybe move to Greenland or someplace like that. Do they care about soccer in Greenland? Why am I thinking about this now? Focus!

Suddenly, a noise from the crowd cuts

through the quiet. Is it an airhorn? Oh no! Not the vuvuzelas! Anything but that!

I glance up and lock eyes with de Gea. Does he hear that awful noise, too? It's like an air-raid siren or something.

Eeeerrrrgggg... eeeerrrrgggg ... eeeerrrrgggg ...

Block it out!

I start my run-up. I've got something special in mind for this one, something old David will never see coming. I plant my left foot, swing my right foot. The noise gets louder, louder ...

Eeeerrrrgggg ...

eeeerrrrgggg ...

eeeerrrrgggg ...

My foot makes contact, the ball rockets forward, the goalie lays out, and ...

I wake up.

I hit the snooze button. Hard.

"Chance!" Mom calls from the kitchen. "Get up! Tryouts are in an hour!"

WHAT'S WORSE THAN tryouts? A coach who schedules them for Labor Day. I mean, who does that?

My mom went bananas when she found out and said we should boycott. I pulled the plug on that one real quick. I can't have my mom marching up and down Columbus Avenue with signs and chanting into a megaphone. Especially not three days before I start 7th grade! Mom said marching and signs are for demonstrations, not boycotts, and that there's a big difference between the two. But for me, they would both end the same way: starting middle school with a whole lot of social problems.

So, I end up telling my mom to go ahead and go to the beach without me. It's not that I don't love the ocean, sun, and all that good stuff, but I live in New York City. Going to the beach means waking up at, like, four in the morning, piling into the car along with my science-nerd sister, Marla, and the sugar-fiend twins, sitting in traffic for hours while Mom's zen is trashed on the Jersey Turnpike. And then, when we finally get to the beach, it's up to me to battle twenty million other people for a spot on the sand. Mom will be in full meditation mode, trying to get her chakras rebalanced or her balance rechakra'ed, or something; Marla will be setting up some kind of solar experiment; and the twins will be chewing through the boardwalk to get to the cotton candy guy.

As much fun as all that sounds, I wanna play soccer this fall more than I wanna try to squeeze in one more beach day before summer ends.

So here I am in Central Park, standing at attention like I'm in boot camp, while Coach Hornbuckle, who's built exactly like a fire hydrant and not much taller than one, marches back and forth in front of us. He's yelling at kids to stand up straight, tie their shoes, and straighten their shin guards. He says "oohrah" a lot and builds our confidence up by calling us "turd-buckets," "puke-rabbits," and "wibble-wabblers" (whatever that means).

Turns out, Coach Hornbuckle scheduled tryouts for Labor Day *on purpose* to weed out recruits (that's us) and their superiors (that's our parents) who aren't committed to the mission. That's the actual word he used: *mission*.

Whatever. Gotta focus! Although, between the 200-degree heat and Coach Hornbuckle's whistle, which he blows so hard it looks like his head is gonna pop off, focusing is even harder than usual.

"Private 27! Let's go!"

That's me: Private 27. I wonder if he'll bother to learn our names if we make the team.

I start dribbling between cones, stop to juggle in a circle painted on the field, and fire a shot into the top-left corner of the goal.

"Private 28! On the hop!"

No "nice shot," no nothing! I'm not a guy who needs a lot of pats on the back or anything, but I can tell already this is gonna to be a lot different from last year, when Coach Sweeney gave us a "Great job, Buddy!" or a "Super effort, Hot Shot," whether we scored a goal or missed on a free kick. I don't mean missed the shot, I mean missed the *ball*. (That wasn't me, by the way.)

When the drills are done, Coach Hornbuckle tells us that the results will be posted on the school bulletin board on Wednesday, the first day of school. Then he gives us a nice thanks-for-coming-out gift of 20 windsprints and 10 burpees before yelling, "Zit Piles, DIIIIIIIIIIS-MISSED!"

So, to sum up, the coach thinks he's a drill sergeant, doesn't know our names, isn't big on encouragement, and is gonna post a giant fail sign in the hallway on the first day of school.

Welcome to middle school, I guess.

YAY! IT'S THE first day of school!

Said no kid ever.

Yay! I'm in the 7th grade now!

Said no kid *my size* ever.

Hurry up! We don't want to be late for the welcome assembly!

Said no kid ever, except for my best friend Ronnie.

We're walking to school together, like we've done every morning since we were ten. Only today, instead of going three blocks uptown to PS 177 Elementary, we're heading three blocks downtown to JFK Middle School. There's not much difference, except that going this way, for some reason, there are a lot more people and piles of dog poop to dribble my ball around. Ronnie is ahead of me, as usual. He's super-neurotic about being on time for everything, even school.

Unfortunately, we don't get hit by a bus or kidnapped by aliens, and we arrive at school just in time for the assembly, which is being called "Ducks

Take Flight!" See, JFK sports teams and, I guess, students in general are called "Ducks."

So, we get herded into the auditorium. But before we can even sit down, they split us up into groups called "teams," which is supposed to—I don't know—make middle school seem like a game of dodgeball or something. A kid with lots of hair gel raises his hand and says, "So, like, if we're on the same team, can we, like, collaborate on tests and stuff?"

The principal, Mr. Sprag, who is almost as skinny as the microphone stand, doesn't like that. He talks about the honor code and makes sure to get Grease Head's name. Something tells me that dude just rocketed to the top of Sprag's most-wanted list.

The worst part, though, is that I'm on Team Widgeon, and Ronnie is on Team Mallard—those are types of ducks, by the way. Since we're on different teams, Ronnie and I have to sit in different sections with a bunch of kids we don't know. No big deal for Ronnie. That kid can talk to anybody—and probably sell them something, too, while he's at it. For me, it's never been quite that easy.

It also means that Ronnie and I aren't in any classes together, and we even have different lunch times. Ronnie's is at 11:30. Mine? 10:45! Who eats lunch at 10:45? Mmm . . . nothing better than soggy tater tots at quarter-to-eleven.

It gets worse. Sprag breaks out the handbook and asks us to recite the Duck Honor Code that's projected on the big screen behind him. We do that, and if there is a more depressing sound than a few hundred kids reading an honor code on the first day of school, I've never heard it.

Then Principal Sprag flips the page and starts reading. And reading. Aaaaaand reading. He's literally reading us the handbook, which would be bad enough if he had a normal voice (which he doesn't) and didn't sound like a sloth on tranquilizers (which he does).

You wouldn't believe how many rules they have in middle school! There's all the normal stuff: no running in the halls, no fighting, etc. But before long, Sprag gets to the freaky stuff.

Like . . .

Rule 12.32: Students may not at any time make marks on the corridor walls by spraying, smearing, spewing, squirting, spritzing, or smashing substances of any kind or color (including transparent) without a signed Decoration Permissions Form (DPF 26b).

Here's the thing about rules like that: The reason they exist is that somebody at some point must have done something really disgusting to those walls. Who that person was and what they smeared, spewed, or smashed, I don't ever wanna know.

Or . . .

Rule 17.03: Students may not eat in the library. Any food or drinks brought into the library must be checked in at the front desk and retrieved upon exit.

That seems normal enough, except that in this case, I know why it was invented—and it's not normal at all. My older sister Marla told me that last year an 8th grader slammed a whole cheeseburger inside a copy of *Lord of the Flies* and put it back on the shelf. Good news: some kid found out, and the librarian got rid of the book. Bad news: that was four months after the burger slam.

How any kid is expected to remember all these rules is beyond me. I've already forgotten half of them by the time the assembly is over. Looks like I'll be spending some quality time with Grease Head in detention this year.

The rest of the day is just as bad. I get lost a gazillion times and am late to every class. Plus, I'm feeling like the shortest kid on the planet, which means I've got to move quickly to avoid getting stepped on in the halls. And did I mention that most of the afternoon I'm starving to death, since I was forced to eat lunch at the crack of dawn?

Ronnie finds me before the last class of the day, while I'm pinballing between a herd of giants in the math wing.

"Chance! Did you make the team?"

I tell him I don't know. I haven't been able to find the bulletin board Coach Hornbuckle said he'd post the tryout results on.

He laughs and hands me a photocopy of a hand-drawn, laminated map of the school. How in the world he managed that, I have no idea, but he's like that. If there's a business opportunity—like selling school maps to traumatized, terrified, totally lost 7th graders—he'll sniff it out.

He tells me not to tell anyone I got it for free, then leads me to the gym, where the bulletin board is.

I can't look, so Ronnie does it for me.

"Okay, 7th grade roster, here we go," he says. The bell rings and kids start flying around. He's still scanning, and my heart is sinking. "I'm sorry, man. You didn't make it. What a crock! We should sue the coach. Or get him a pair of glasses. Unbelievable!"

I can't say anything. I feel like I just got punched in the stomach. Ronnie tries to cheer me up.

"But, dude, think about how much time we'll have for business! Maybe we can finally get that pigeon poop predictor off the ground!"

The hallway is thinning out as kids disappear into classrooms. Ronnie takes off down the hall, and I trudge slowly to my last class of the day, English. Mr. Biesanz says that this fall, we'll be studying some of the greatest tragedies ever written.

Perfect.

THAT NIGHT, MOM goes bonkers. She's pacing around the kitchen, doing calm-breathing exercises, and asking me how in the world I didn't make the team. Like I can answer that. I think I had a pretty good tryout, but I guess Coach Hornbuckle didn't agree. Mom notices my school directory on the table. Her eyes get big. I make a dive for it, but her arm strikes like a cobra, and she starts rifling through the directory and dialing a number like a madwoman . . . like a madwoman somehow doing yoga breathing exercises.

With a phone in her hand, my mom is a force of nature. Principal? Mayor? Pope? Give her two bars, half a battery, and ten minutes, and she'll have them on the other end, whether they like it or not.

Not surprisingly, Mom gets Coach Hornbuckle's cell number—or walkie-talkie frequency.

There is absolutely no way this ends well. I'll never play soccer again. I'll definitely have to change schools, maybe states. I may never leave my room again. I seem to remember a dream about moving to Greenland. Doesn't sound like a bad idea right now.

Coach Hornbuckle answers, and he and Mom get into an instant barking match.

Then something weird happens. Mom suddenly gets quiet. I peek through my fingers and see that she is smiling, which makes no sense. Then, she actually *thanks* the coach and hangs up.

"You didn't make the 7th grade team," she says.

Yah. Thanks. I'm aware.

"You made the 8th grade team!"

My jaw drops. *What?!?*

"Yes! I knew there had to be a mistake or something. By the way, the coach called you a new recruit. What's that about?"

I just stare at her.

"What's the matter, Chance? Aren't you excited?!?"

No, Mom. I am not excited. In fact, this is the worst news ever! She doesn't get it, so I have to explain to her that I'll get stomped on at practice and never get off the bench during games. That the guys on the 8th-grade team are all like seven-feet tall! She tells me I'm silly, then hugs me and says how proud she is.

I should have just gone to the beach on tryout day. Maybe it's not too late for Greenland . . .

WE HAVE TWO practices that week, and they go pretty much how I thought they would. Coach puts me in the back of the stretching lines. I'm last in line for every drill and even last in line for the fountain at water breaks. Talk about the low guy on the totem pole! If there were a ditch to be dug with a spoon, or a toilet to be cleaned with a toothbrush, I'm pretty sure I'd be the first one picked for *those* jobs.

When we finally start scrimmaging, things don't get much better. The other guys are giants, and they aren't happy about a 7th grader being on the team. I hardly ever touch the ball. Basically, I get ignored, unless I'm getting slammed into the dirt.

Coach Hornbuckle is totally tough, too. Everything is "Yes, Sir," "No, Sir," and if you happen to forget that, you get a bunch of burpees to jog your memory. He's dropped the whole "Private 27" thing, but he's replaced it with something worse: nicknames. Not cool ones, like the pros have: El Gato, Becks, the Bison, or El Niño. We get super-embarrassing ones, the kind drill sergeants in movies give to recruits on the first day of boot camp. Take our backline, for example: Walt, Zach, Calvin, and Jungo are now Tuna Cart, Toejam, Pitstain, and Cheese Wagon.

Finally, Saturday rolls around and it's time to actually play a game. Or, in my case, watch a game from the bench like a chump. We're playing the Soho Middle School Tigers. It's early September, and it is *hot.* Like, the kind of hot where taxi exhaust fumes feel like a blast of cool air.

Soho isn't anything great, but they're in way better shape than we are. Midway through the second half, two of their midfielders grab a rebound, break away, and our guys are so wrecked they look like they're running in quicksand. Our defense is spent. They're gasping and wheezing and trying to get back into position. Our goalie Brick is the size of a minivan, but even he has no chance. 1-0, Soho.

Artie, one of our forwards, goes down holding his leg. Bash, the other one, actually barfs on the field.

"Medic!" Sergeant Hornbuckle yells, which he does whenever somebody gets hurt, like he's the star of an old war movie or something. Then he turns to the bench. "Shag Carpet, you're in."

Gustavo (Coach calls him "Shag Carpet" because of his hair) hops up from the bench and sprints onto the field. But he only makes it a few steps before *he* goes down, too, grabbing his calf and howling like a werewolf.

"Dadgummit! Medic!" Coach roars. "Frodinho! Get warm!"

Yeah, that's me. Because I'm short. Hilarious.

As for getting warm, no problem there.

I'm roasting! I get up and start jogging on the sidelines.

There's a sharp whisper from behind me. It's my mom. She's down on the ground in a full split. I tell her to get up, that she can't do yoga here. If Coach sees us, we'll both get thrown in the brig. I don't actually know what the brig is, but Coach is always threatening to throw us in it.

Mom shushes me and says that Coach doesn't know the first thing about stretching. The problem, she says, is that everyone is cramping.

"If you go out there right now, in this heat, you'll cramp, too," she says. "I'm not leaving until you do this stretch."

I do it. I feel like an idiot, but I know there's no use arguing with her when she's in yoga mode.

"Frodinho!" Coach yells. "What in all the blazes are you doing?"

I hop up. Mom is gone and Coach hasn't seen her—thank goodness.

"I'm ready."

He glares at me. His face is the color of a fire truck. A really angry fire truck.

"I'm ready, *Sir*," I say.

He says I'm in for Pippi Longstocking (that's Artie, because of his freckles, I assume). He tells me to mark Soho's number 12 tight and if I manage to get my foot on the ball, to push it forward to Puke Cannon (that's Bash, I think because his last name is Buchannon, although he did just barf too).

And just like that, I'm in the game. There are only five minutes left, and it takes two of them for me to even feel like I'm playing soccer, not just trying to stay alive at Jurassic Park.

Suddenly, Hugo slide tackles one of their forwards, and the ball pops right to me at midfield. Everything goes quiet, like it usually does when I've got my foot on the ball. I see three defenders back-peddling, the fourth one, a scary guy with a moustache—like, a full-on moustache!— is coming at me hard, smiling like a raptor. I don't see their midfielders behind me, but I know they're coming, too.

I fake right, step over, and head left. The moustache dude gasps, but I'm gone. The three remaining defenders are all out of breath, but the one on the left is really panting and has his hands on his knees. That's my guy.

I dribble hard, straight up the middle. In the corner of my eye, I see Bash working up the right sideline.

Stay onside, I think.

When the middle defender breaks for me, I cut hard left and punch it between my guy's legs. He ignores the ball and comes right at me. He'll foul me, if I let him, but I don't want a free kick. I get low, duck my shoulder, and he goes bowling right past me.

I'm in the box now, and I've got the goalie's full attention. I fake a shot with my right foot, and he falls for it. With my left, I fire across the box . . . where Bash is charging in with every last bit of energy he's got. The ball catches his right foot in stride. One touch. Goal.

Now all the sound comes back into my ears. I join the big knot of my teammates jumping up and down around Bash. I come up to maybe their armpits, and that's a bad place to be on a day like this.

But, hey, at least we didn't lose!

Oohrah?

Game	Result	My Goals	My Assists	Team Barfs
JFK Ducks vs. Soho Tigers	T 1-1	0	1	1

THE NEXT DAY is crazy hot, too, and I should be
working on a book report for our summer reading
assignment, but there's one problem: I haven't
read the book. I figured if I read a book way back
in summer, how would I remember anything when
the report was due? I make my way onto the fire
escape—the only quiet part of our apartment—with
my library copy of *The Adventures of Tom Sawyer*. I
read the first sentence four times.

Not happening.

Need to get some brain juices flowing.

According to Mrs. Hurts, our PE teacher, exercise

is the best way to do that. So I grab my soccer ball, and I'm out the door.

I stop and get an Italian ice from the lady on the corner. That soft, delicious frozen mess in a paper cup is by far one of the best things about hot days in New York City. And, like everything else that's good here, there's a line usually up the block for it. But in case you've never had an Italian ice, it's worth the wait. Trust me.

Of course, there are other things about hot days in the city that aren't so great.

I'm dribbling my ball up Columbus Avenue, and blue stuff is running all down my arm, when I see a sign that says "Andy's Exotic Animal Emporium." It must be new.

When I walk in, it takes me a minute to adjust to how dark it is inside. Before I know what's happening, a giant black bird swoops down out of nowhere, snatches my half-eaten ice, and disappears again. Did I just get mugged by a raven?

I must've said this out loud because I hear a voice beside me say, "She's actually a crow." Standing right next to me is a girl with short hair and a giant smile. The big, black bird is sitting on her shoulder—eating my Italian ice!

"I'm Andy," she says. "And this is Bonnie."

The huge beak is right next to Andy's cheek, but she doesn't seem scared at all.

"She's named after Bonnie Parker—the bank robber."

Makes sense.

I feel like asking for my ice back, but it only cost a dollar, and I don't think getting my face pecked off is worth that.

Turns out, Andy's new in town and she goes to my school. She gives me a tour of the shop. It's her dad's, but she

works there—and it's named for her! I can't even get my coach to call me by my real name!

It doesn't take long to figure out that this place is the real deal. Every glass case I look into contains some exotic animal I've only read about in books. Instead of the usual boring goldfish and hamsters, they've got sea dragons, African pygmy hedgehogs, albino snakes, and bird-eating tarantulas! I think Andy must be the luckiest kid in New York City.

In the reptile section, there's a bright green thing with bulging eyeballs sitting on a branch. And here's the freaky thing: It's staring at me with one eye, while the other eye is locked onto a cricket crawling on a nearby branch. I think, *Being able to look in two different directions at the same time would sure come in handy on the soccer field!*

Then, all of a sudden, the green thing's tongue shoots out, nabs the cricket, and starts munching away, cool as a cucumber.

"*Chamaeleo calyptratus,*" Andy says.

I tell her sorry, I don't speak Klingon. She says, no, that's its scientific name.

"Its common name is Veiled Chameleon," she says.

A chameleon! Right then and there, I decide that I've gotta have him.

Andy says he costs forty bucks, but with the glass case and all the stuff I'd need, it's gonna be more like $150. Doesn't matter. I'm sold. One problem: I've got about 12¢ to my name. Maybe Andy's dad will knock a dollar off for the Italian ice.

I lean in close and tell the chameleon I'll be back for him soon.

NOW I NEED to raise some cash. Luckily, I know just the guy, and I know right where to find him.

Ronnie is in the rec room of Sunset Terrace, an old folks' home his parents made him volunteer at after he got in trouble for "borrowing" traffic cones and renting them to people who didn't want to lose their parking spots on the street. That was a couple of years ago, but Ronnie still goes every week. They love him down there.

$150

$125

$100

$75

$50

$25

It's Silver Screen Sunday, so the rec room is set up like a movie theater. Ronnie is stationed next to the old-timey popcorn machine. No, he doesn't sell the popcorn to the old folks, but if any of them offer him a tip for good service or extra butter, well, there's no harm in that, right?

Ronnie puts me to work right away, delivering bags of popcorn and running to the kitchen for more salt and butter. The room gets dark and quiet once the movie begins. He and I sit in the back with a bag of popcorn each.

I try to talk to Ronnie about how I can raise $150, but I keep getting shushed by the audience. Halfway through the bag, I reach for the glass of soda next to me, but then a lot of bad things happen.

First, the soda doesn't taste like soda. Second, something bumps into my mouth from inside the glass.

It's a bunch of teeth smiling at me!

I spew the water all over the lady in front of me. The guy beside me, who everybody calls "Big Al," starts laughing—and his mouth doesn't have any teeth.

Barf! I'm chugging Big Al's denture-storage water!

Ronnie catches up with me in the bathroom, where I'm gargling hand sanitizer. I tell him I'm suing him for damages: $150. That night, I brush and floss like there's no tomorrow.

THINGS ARE LOOKING up this week. I get an extension on the summer reading book report from Mr. Biesanz by telling him that the book has triggered some painful childhood memories for me. I don't even know what *Tom Sawyer* is about really, but as most kids know, using the word "triggered" with adults can get you out of a lot of things—even book reports!

It's not that I don't like reading, and this book is supposed to have a bunch of action and murders and stuff. The problem is that I haven't gotten to any of that yet. So far, all Tom's done is get a kid to paint a fence for him. Super exciting stuff.

Soccer practice goes better this week, too. Coach Hornbuckle is still a nutcase, but the guys on the team act a lot cooler with me after the Soho game.

Another piece of good news: I manage to raise $9.90 for the chameleon fund by selling empty soda cans to my sister Marla for 18¢ apiece.

Why is my sister buying empty soda cans? Well, first, you need to understand something about Marla: She is a science genius (*cough—nerd—cough*), and she's always doing these weird science experiments. Not even for school—just for fun! Like I said: *nerd*. Although for all her smarts, she still can't figure out how to cure the case of hiccups she's had since last Christmas. I got a Messi jersey, Marla got a permanent case of the hiccups. Santa really is magic.

Anyway, this week, Marla's working on something to do with the center of gravity, and every flat surface of our apartment is covered with soda cans standing at weird angles. It's actually a little spooky. But at 18¢ a can, who am I to question science?

THIS WEEKEND'S GAME is against the Harlem
Aces, and they've got this kid, Albert something,
who is at least 99% legs. Seriously. He's like one
of those daddy longlegs spiders, except with two
legs, not eight.

From the moment the game kicks off, this guy
is killing us. He's completely un-tackle-able and
sneaky fast. He's one of those guys who doesn't
look like he's running hard, but every stride
eats up like five yards, and, next thing you know,
he's past you.

We're down 2-0 at the half, and Coach spends

the whole halftime drawing up trap plays for the fullbacks and reminding the midfielders what a slide tackle is supposed to look like—all while threatening us with court-martials and the brig.

Once the second half starts, we're right back where we started. Every time Walt, Zach, Calvin, and Jungo collapse down on Spidey, he pops a quick step-over, fires the ball through their legs, then lopes right through them like they're standing still. Anybody who goes for a tackle on him gets hopped over like a speed bump.

But one thing's different about the second half: *me*. To everybody's surprise (especially mine), Coach puts me in for Artie. At first, I end up doing way more watching than I'd like, waiting for a pass so we can get some offense going. *But how can we score if we can't get the ball away from Spidey?*

Finally, midway through the second half, Spiderlegs pegs a shot off the crossbar, and Zach gets the rebound. I'm streaking down the middle, and Zach chips the ball right over the center-full's head—and onto my foot. It's just me and the goal—well, and the goalie, of course, but I'll take those odds any day.

FWOOSH! Something blows past me from behind, and I realize two things at the same time: 1. The FWOOSH was Spiderlegs. And, 2. I don't have the ball anymore.

I'm crushed, not to mention exhausted. I grab my knees for a second, just to catch my breath, when I hear a hiccup and spot Marla in the bleachers. She's got a big science textbook open and is working on balancing her soda cans on top of each other in weird ways. At first I'm annoyed. Why come to the game if you're only gonna do gravity research in bleachers?!?

And then it hits me! A kid with legs that long has got to have a crazy high center of gravity. Tackling him low won't do any good, but a nudge up top, well, that might be an issue for him!

I gotta get the word out, but one problem: no timeouts in soccer.

I shout to Coach Hornbuckle that I'm gonna switch from forward to rogue, which will let me go anywhere on the field without wrecking the formation. I know that if this doesn't work, I'll be on the bench (if not in the brig) next game, but the clock is ticking and we're down 2-nothing!

I spend the next few minutes tracking the ball, which is usually in the possession of Spiderlegs, of course. But my main goal is to whisper two words to everybody on our team: "Wobbly Top." At first, nobody knows what I'm talking about. I realize I'm gonna have to demo this strategy myself.

At that moment, the ball rolls out of bounds

on our side of the field, and we're setting up to defend the in-bound. Just as one of their guys is throwing it in toward Spiderlegs, I make a break on the ball and give Spidey a healthy nudge with my shoulder—not enough to knock him down and draw a card, I hope. . . .

He bounces off me like a big old rubber band, stumbling, flailing, trying to get his legs back under him. I yell, "Wobbly Top!" and I see my teammates' eyes light up.

No more slide tackles for Spiderlegs to hop over! Now he's got to keep his balance, and that's no small feat when you're all legs!

Suddenly, we're in control again. While Spiderlegs is getting bumped and bopped—with us shouting "Wobbly Top!" each time—Hugo weaves past a couple of defenders, hits me running down the sideline, and I chip the ball into the box . . . where Bash is waiting to slam home a header.

After that, it's like we cracked the code. A couple guys pick up yellow cards for toppling old Wobbly a little too hard, but Coach just calls it "good, hard-nosed scrumming." (I think he makes up half these words.) He doesn't smile or anything, but I read his forehead veins and can tell he's dropped from "raging rhinoceros" to "grumpy badger" on the anger scale, which is pretty good for him.

And most importantly, we win! Nick popped a rebound in, and Bash got his second on a penalty kick, after one of Soho's defenders got mad and used the Wobbly Top on him. 3-2, JFK Ducks!

I'm expecting an earful from Coach for my on-the-fly decision, but instead, he gives me a promotion. He says, "Solid field tactical awareness, Frodinho. I'm promoting you to Lance Corporal." I don't know what he's talking about, as usual, but I hope it means I'll be starting next game.

Game	Result	My Goals	My Assists	Tops Wobbled
JFK Ducks vs. Harlem Aces	W 3–2	0	1	1

IN MOST SCHOOLS, PE stands for Physical
Education. Dodgeball, jump rope, basketball, that
kind of thing, right? Not at JFK Middle. Here, I'm
pretty sure PE stands for Peak Embarrassment.

It starts that Monday. Mrs. Hurts brings in this
super-skinny lady named Miss Martina. As in Miss
Martina's School of Dance on 70th and Broadway.
This can't be good.

Miss Martina wheels in a TV and plays a video
of people in tuxedos and gowns twirling each other
around. We're all sitting on the gym floor, and
Mrs. Hurts is stalking around like a tiger ready to

pounce on anyone dumb enough to laugh or crack a joke. When it's over, Miss Martina bows (an actual bow, like she did something important) and tells us that we are about to "embark upon a journey into the magical world of ballroom dancing."

Oh, this is really, really not good.

I mean, dancing is bad enough. Dancing with another person is worse. Ballroom dancing with another person . . . they don't even have a word for that. For one thing, I'm shorter than almost every girl in PE, and for another, I've got a weird foot.

See, I was born with a club foot, which is not as cool as it sounds. It doesn't mean my foot was a weapon an ogre would use. Or that I was born to tear up the dance floor in clubs. In fact, my right foot used to be turned all the way in, so that it pointed at my left ankle! I had to wear this crazy brace that looked like a snowboard—for years! I was little, so I don't remember it that well, but I still always feel like my feet are somehow . . . *off*. Maybe that's why I like soccer so much. When I'm dribbling a ball, everybody's looking at the ball, not my feet. I think magicians call it "misdirection."

These days, my feet look pretty normal . . . but ballroom dancing? Forget about it.

Like everything else in middle school, it seems I've got no choice in the matter (shocker!), so until I can think of a way out of this, I've gotta go with it. I get paired up with Samantha Durgan, who is an 8th grader and . . . well . . . things get ugly real quick.

Not only is Samantha peeved, but I see my teammate Artie giving me a death glare from across the gym. He's been in love with Samantha since the beginning of time. I'm pretty sure I've taken the guy's starting spot on the soccer team, and now I'm gonna be dancing with Samantha every day this semester? That won't end well for me.

Long story short, I manage to pull Miss Martina aside and explain to her that I've got a physical, um, issue with my feet, and in order to prevent me from injuring myself and others, I should really be paired up with someone a little shorter. Someone with smaller feet. Someone like, say, Laverne Sneedly . . . who happens to be Artie's partner.

Miss Martina gives me a real puppy dog look that makes me wanna barf, but she makes the switch. Artie's thrilled. Laverne throws a fit. I'm pretty sure she's faking it, though, since she's always pinching me or sticking her pencil in my hair—and that means a girl has a crush on you, right?

It's gonna be a long semester in Peak Embarrassment class, but at least I've done Artie a solid. Don't say I never did nothin' for ya, Pippi Longstocking!

ON WEDNESDAY, ONE of my maniac little brothers, Zephyr, has to go to the dentist. Ever since he and Zane watched *Zombie Dentist 3: Drillfinger's Revenge* at a sleepover last Halloween, Z^2's trips to the dentist's office have become total nightmares for the entire family. Of course, since their diet consists of 99 percent pure sugar,

those nightmares happen pretty regularly.

It's totally unfair. When I was their age, I'd be lucky to get beet-juice sweetened pudding, which is as bad as it sounds. Marla, for her part, always complains about how good I had it compared to when she was little. I don't know how that's possible, unless Mom just fed her houseplants and tree bark.

Anyway, Mom's only chance of getting out of the dentist's office alive and without Z^2 in jail is to take them one at a time. Marla has jiu jitsu on Wednesdays—How she can do jiu jitsu while hiccupping every five seconds, I have no idea—so Zane has to come to soccer practice with me that day. No way I'll be able to keep an eye on him and the ball (Man, those chameleon eyes would really come in handy!), so I call Ronnie. I tell him I'll call off the denture lawsuit if he'll come to practice and keep Zane from bum-rushing the ice cream guy or anybody dumb enough to chew gum within smelling range.

Practice that day goes well. We're in better shape now, and it looks like I've got the starting forward spot locked down. After practice, I notice Coach Hornbuckle and Ronnie having some kind of serious conversation. Then, they shake hands and Coach Hornbuckle hands Ronnie five bucks!

Okay, what in the world could that be about?

Ronnie's not talking, though. He says he's on a secret mission, something about *reconnaissance*.

I swear, that kid is gonna be a millionaire by age 14. Maybe I should wait until then to sue him.

THE NEXT TWO days at practice, we spend all of our time learning a new defensive formation that Coach Hornbuckle calls "Twin Buster." Apparently, Washington Heights Middle—that's who we're playing on Saturday—has a couple of twin wings who are so in-tune with each other, it's like they share a brain. How Coach knows this, I have no idea.

The game plan is for our guys to basically split into two mini-teams, each focusing on one half of the field—the wings, in particular. Seems like this is gonna leave the middle wide open, but Coach doesn't ask my opinion.

Saturday rolls around, and it's finally cooling off and feeling like fall in New York. That means more leaves on the ground and hopefully less heat-stroke barf on the field. Washington Heights shows up to the field, and I can't believe my eyes. The twins are tiny—like, smaller than me! They've got enormous heads and identical bowl haircuts. These guys can't be that dangerous. They look like a couple of bobbleheads!

They are completely identical, too, and their jerseys are too big for them. It looks ridiculous, but when the game starts, I start to think there might be some strategy behind it. One of them is number 8, the other is number 9, but with their giant jerseys tucked into their shorts, you can only see the tops of their numbers—which means you can't tell them apart by their numbers either!

So now we've got these two bobbleheads running around like crazy, and there is zero chance of telling them apart. Which, as you can imagine, totally wrecks our game plan.

When we are on defense, we are chasing these two munchkins around, crashing into each other, tripping over ourselves, and generally looking like idiots. And these two guys—one of them is named Greg and the other is Craig (pronounced "Creg", according to a large-headed family in the stands)—never say a word. But it's true about their telepathic link. They always know where the other one is gonna be and what the other one is gonna do. They're lobbing crossers to each other non-stop as they work their way down the field, switching sides over and over again, and almost always getting good shots on goal.

Thankfully, Washington Heights has a Swiss cheese defense, so we're scoring, too.

At halftime, it's 4-4. I've notched two assists and gotten my first goal of the season on a nice feeder from Nick right up the middle of the field.

Coach Hornbuckle spends all of halftime barking at the referee about uniform regulations, but what can the ref do? The Egg Twins have their jerseys tucked in, like they're supposed to. Is it their fault they aren't very tall?

That leaves it to us, the players, to sort out the second-half strategy. The guys are arguing about how to tell the twins apart so that each mini-team can cover the guy they're supposed to be covering.

That's when I speak up.

"Um." It's the only thing that comes out at first, because I'm pretty nervous. I never say a word when the older guys are talking strategy, so when I say something—even something as dumb as "um"— it manages to get their attention.

"I think there's a better way," I say. "I've got little brothers—*twins*. And, here's the thing, everybody is always trying to treat them exactly the same. They are used to getting equal amounts of everything."

Nick's like, "So?"

I explain that our game plan against the Eggs is playing right into what they're used to. In my experience, if you wanna to drive a couple of twins insane, you do the opposite: you pay lots of attention to one, and zero attention to the other one.

I ask Hugo for a piece of gum. (He's always chomping on a massive wad of some kind of high-tech, nuclear-green electrolyte gum.) He gives one over, and I tell the guys my plan. I hope it works, because we don't have another one.

The second half kicks off, and I make a beeline for the nearest Egg. When I get close enough, I spit the gum into my hand and stick it to his back. I don't know if it's Greg or Craig, but it doesn't matter. What matters is that now we can tell them apart.

The defense totally focuses on Gum Egg and leaves No-Gum Egg mostly alone. And, as I hoped, the invisible wires that connect their brains completely short circuit.

Gum Egg is feeling like the bigger threat, which makes him feel more important than No-Gum Egg. No-Gum, on the other hand, is feeling neglected and less important.

Total. Twin. Meltdown.

Now, whenever there's a break in the action, like when the ball goes out of bounds or there's a foul, the Eggs are arguing, their enormous heads bouncing up and down like crazy. They are completely off their game, and the rest of the team just falls apart.

We grab three quick goals, go into keep-away mode for the rest of the game, and cruise to our second win in a row.

We're in second place with five games to go before the championship.

MANHATTAN 8TH GRADE 3-A LEAGUE
WEEK 3 STANDINGS

Team	Wins	Losses	Ties	Goals For	Goals Against
Greenwich Dragons	3	0	0	12	4
JFK Ducks	2	0	1	11	7
West End Secondary FC	2	1	0	9	7
Harlem Aces	1	1	0	6	5
Washington Heights Rams	1	2	1	9	12
East Village Wizards	0	0	3	0	0
Soho Tigers	0	1	1	2	5
Battery Bruisers	0	2	1	0	3
CUAC	0	2	1	2	8

Oh, and I'm leading the team in assists with 5, and third in goals with 2. I didn't know about it until after the game, when Artie, who has taken on a kind of assistant-coach role now, checks his clipboard and lets me know. He even gives me a little pat on the head. I feel a little bit like a puppy. But, hey, it's better than getting squashed!

Game	Result	My Goals	My Assists	Pieces of Gum I Owe Hugo
JFK Ducks vs. Washington Heights Rams	W 7-4	2	3	1

I BARELY MAKE it to English class, thanks to a little issue that took place in Peak Embarrassment.

At the end of the class, Miss Martina gathered us all around to make an *important announcement*. Her eye makeup was all smeared, which I think means she'd been crying. She looked like a zombie in high heels.

But she wasn't sad or anything. She had what Mom calls "happy tears," because some anonymous person donated enough money for every kid taking ballroom dance to get a new pair of dance shoes.

Gee, thanks, kind, anonymous person. Just what

I've always wanted: a pair of black leather clunkers with soles so slick we can basically ice skate across the basketball court. The girls were gonna be getting sparkly, high-heeled things, and most of them seemed pretty excited as we all lined up to get fitted.

Like I said, I'm self-conscious about my feet, so I wasn't looking forward to breaking them out in front of the entire class. So, I made sure I was at the back of the fitting line.

Which is why I'm late to English. Miss Martina was nice enough to write me a note, so at least Mr.

Biesanz doesn't give me detention or anything. I head for the only seat available, but before I can sit down, something brown and furry with a long tail scurries out from under the chair.

I must've shrieked, because the entire class is looking at me. I glance back down to see the thing crawl into the front pocket of the overalls that the kid in front of me is wearing. And I see that the kid is Andy, the girl from the exotic pet store.

Mr. Biesanz asks one of those teachery questions: "Mr. Striker, is there something alarming about Mr. Loman's search for the American Dream that you wish to share with the class?"

Andy's eyes are huge. She's afraid I'm gonna rat her out about, well, her rat. But Andy seems like a cool kid, and, besides, I've got a chameleon to think about.

On her desk I see the play we're supposed to be reading.

"Yes, of course!" I say. "It is alarming that he dies."

I haven't gotten around to reading the play just yet, but thank goodness the writer gave the whole story away in the title, *Death of a Salesman*. I just hope this Mr. Loman guy is the salesman who dies. Wait, that sounds kind of dark.

Anyway, it works. Mr. Biesanz gives a big sigh and stares out the window, like he's lost in thought. He does this a lot—he's super melodramatic—and this time, it gives me enough time to sit down and disappear. When Mr. Biesanz comes back to Planet Earth, he starts in on the tragedy of it all, and I think maybe I'm about to see my second teacher in a row start sobbing.

Andy smiles and drops a couple Cheerios into her pocket. She owes me one. Wonder what the no-rat-on-the-rat discount on chameleons is. . . .

PRACTICE THIS WEEK is all about ball movement. We're playing the East Village Wizards, who haven't won a game yet, but they haven't lost one yet either. They are 0-0-3. Three ties! Coach Hornbuckle says that they don't have much of an offense, but that their defense is stout. In fact, all of their games have ended in scoreless ties. How boring!

From what Coach says, their central defender is an absolute beast. He's not the biggest or the fastest, but he's always in the right place at the right time. He idolizes Maldini, an old Italian soccer star, according to Coach. (I've never heard of him.)

So we run attacking drills, and after practice on Thursday, Coach calls Bash and me over. He hands us each a folder stamped "Top Secret" in big red letters and tells us that Sun Tzu teaches us to "know thine enemy."

Why Coach is getting all churchy on us with "thine," or who this Sun Tzu guy is, I have no idea. But I'm not in the mood for wind sprints, so I just give him a "Yes sir!" and head for home.

At the edge of Central Park, who is waiting for me but Andy, with two fat hedgehogs on leashes. Seems weird, but people in New York City do a lot of weird things.

Andy introduces me to the hedgehogs, Ground and Pound, who are munching on sidewalk popcorn that was probably popped in the eighties. She thanks me for not squealing on her in English class. I'm pretty sure I did squeal a little, but not in the way she means, so I ask her if maybe her dad will knock a few bucks off the chameleon for me.

She says that she, Ground, and Pound will have a word with him and see what they can do. Then she sees my Top Secret folder, and she's gotta know what's in it. I make sure Coach isn't anywhere around and open it up. There's a note inside that reads:

The following intelligence report
has been prepared for Alpha Wolf
by Iron E. Intelligence Services.
The information herein is top
secret. Sharing it will result in
immediate court marshalling and
other punishments. Should this
fall into enemy hands, Iron E.
Intelligence Services will deny
all knowledge of it. Destroy this
note after reading.

Wow! Sounds pretty official! Andy is going bonkers to see what else there is. Even the hedgehogs have taken a break from fossilized popcorn to look up at us.

I smell an opportunity. I have no idea what's in the file either, but that's not the point. I've got something to sell!

I channel my inner Ronnie and tell Andy that this is high-level stuff, that I'm not so sure she's ready for this kind of thing. She agrees to knock ten bucks off the chameleon and throw in a month of free crickets if she can see the rest. Deal! We shake on it, find a bench, and dive into the file.

It's all about the Wizards' central defender, Eduardo Capriani, who goes by "*Il Capitan*." He copied that nickname from his hero Maldini, who was a famous backline player for AC Milan and the Italian national team in the 80s and 90s, according to the file. There's all kinds of stuff in here about Eduardo: shoe size, jersey number (3, like Maldini), tendencies on the field—even his favorite food. It's pizza. Not sure if that was Maldini's or not, but he was Italian, so chances are good.

Andy seems pretty let down, but when we get to a picture of mini-*Il Capitan* that's paper-clipped to the back of the folder, she says, "Hey! I know that kid!"

She says that he came into the exotic pet shop last week, asking about what kind of animals eat pigeons. There are a bunch, apparently: hawks, owls, falcons, cats. But Andy's shop doesn't have any of them. Raptors—that's what they call killer birds, she says—are too expensive to keep in stock, and cats aren't exotic enough.

So *Il Capitan* got mad, yelled at everyone in

the shop for not doing something about the rats with wings that are taking over the city, and left in a huff.

"Why does he hate pigeons so much?" I ask.

Andy replies, "For the same reason that most people act like they hate a certain kind of animal: he's afraid of them."

I sense a plan hatching in my brain and decide to walk Andy back to her shop for supplies.

IT'S GAME DAY, and my shorts are baggier than usual. Coach Hornbuckle notes that my uniform isn't shipshape, but luckily, he doesn't check my pockets, both of which are packed with high-grade birdseed from Alaska. I don't know what's so special about it, but Andy warned me not to open the bag until absolutely necessary. So I waited until just before kickoff.

When the game starts, I, Chance Striker, am suddenly King of the Pigeons. As soon as I begin running, pigeons come out of nowhere and start circling above me. Two minutes into the game, they start landing on the field to tussle over the bits that spill out of my pockets! This stuff is like a high-powered pigeon magnet!

Il Capitan is looking like *Ill Capitan*. His eyes are wide, his face is green, and he wants nothing to do with me and my army of "rats with wings." On my first touch, I head straight for him, the feathered squadron behind me. He just screams, sprints backwards, and crashes directly into the goalie. Easiest goal I've ever scored!

One problem: I've got to keep moving. I realize real fast that if I stop, I'm gonna turn into one big birdfeeder!

So, the whole first half, I'm running around like a maniac, scoring like Ronaldo, and by the time the whistle blows, I'm completely spent. I make a beeline for the port-o-potties and dump the seeds down the toilet. When I come out, there are about two thousand pigeons waiting for me, and they don't look happy.

Fortunately, my cleats have collected a few bits of seed. I dump them out and make a run for it. When I get back to the sideline, the second half is already underway. I sit on the bench for the rest of the game, but I've got three goals and an assist already, and we cruise to a 6-nil win.

Il Capitan is nowhere to be found.

After the game, Coach pulls me aside and gives me a funny look. I can't tell if he's mad or happy—he's the kind of guy who turns red either way. But this time, I'm prepared.

"You may advance and be absolutely

irresistible, if you make for the enemy's weak points," I say. That's a Sun Tzu quote I picked up the night before, thanks to Google and several attempts at getting the spelling of Sun Tzu's name right. Then I add: "Sir!"

He slaps me on the back, gives me an "oohrah!," and promotes me to corporal right then and there. Frodo Baggins had the One Ring. Frodinho? I'm The Lord of the Pigeons.

Game	Result	My Goals	My Assists	NYC Pigeons Who Suddenly Want to Move to Alaska
JFK Ducks vs. East Village Wizards	W 6-0	3	1	148

MANHATTAN 8TH GRADE 3-A LEAGUE
WEEK 4 STANDINGS

Team	Wins	Losses	Ties	Goals For	Goals Against
Greenwich Dragons	4	0	0	23	5
JFK Ducks	3	0	1	17	7
West End Secondary FC	3	1	0	15	12
Soho Tigers	1	1	1	3	5
Harlem Aces	1	2	0	11	11
Washington Heights Rams	1	2	1	9	12
East Village Wizards	0	1	3	0	6
Battery Bruisers	0	3	1	0	4
CUAC	0	3	1	3	19

GOOD NEWS! THE chameleon fund is up to $33, and the price is down to $140, thanks to my deal with Andy. Marla has moved on to other experiments, which means the soda-can drive is over. But I've managed to squirrel away a few bucks here and there. Plus, Halloween is coming, and that's always a good money-maker for Ronnie and me.

Yeah, we might be a little old for trick-or-treating, but here's

$140!

$125

$100

$75

$50

$25

the thing: Ronnie and I know all the doormen in the neighborhood, and we know all the apartments to hit in order to get the good stuff: Snickers, Reeses, Hersheys—and not the minis. I'm talking about the folks who hand out the full-sizers! We can sell that stuff at school for a quarter of what they cost in the bodega and still make out like bandits. Last year, we made $43 each!

That's a few weeks away, and I've got lots of soccer to think about. We are in second place behind Greenwich Middle, who wins the championship every year, and that's a big deal. Our school, JFK Middle, hasn't even made it to the championship game in like ten years. None of the guys on the team even seem to notice when some comedian scribbles S's on our posters, where the D for Ducks should be. Happens every year, they tell me.

There has to be some rule about that in the handbook, but I don't have time to look it up. I gotta get this *Tom Sawyer* book read. My plan is to spend the entire day Sunday on the fire escape, which is the only Z^2-free zone of our apartment. I don't bring anything with me except the book, a blanket, and a bag of snacks. The idea is to limit distractions, but the snacks turn out to be a bad idea.

See, the couple that lives below us put a Christmas tree on their fire escape and haven't moved it. That was *three years ago*. Since then, it's lost all of its needles but has collected an unbelievable amount of other things: leaves, plastic bags, newspapers, even an old black boot—and that's just the non-living stuff!

So, here I am, sitting in what's supposed to be my own little quiet zone and grinding through *Tom Sawyer*, which actually isn't too bad. I'm munching on kale chips, which are gross, but they're all I could find. Not only are kale chips *not* chips, they make a huge mess. For every handful I get in my mouth, twice that much ends up floating down to the landing below me.

Suddenly, right when Tom and Huck are sneaking around in a haunted house, I hear this growl from below me . . . a *hungry* growl. The Trashmas Tree starts shaking and snarling! I already know stuff lives in it: pigeons, squirrels, maybe even a rat or something. But a something that *growls*??? I'm out. I dump the rest of the kale chips on the tree, hoping they will either distract or disgust whatever ferocious beast is in there, and tumble through the window onto the living room floor.

So much for the book report. I'd rather get a zero than get eaten!

AFTER TUESDAY'S PRACTICE, Coach Hornbuckle delivers another pair of Top Secret folders to Bash and me. Bash makes a little motion with his head, and I follow him out of Central Park.

Bash asks me about the note in the front of the folder, which says that it's been prepared for someone named "Alpha Wolf" by something called "Iron E. Intelligence Services." I say that Alpha Wolf must be some kind of codename for Coach Hornbuckle, but I have no idea about the rest of it. All I know is these intel briefs have sure come in handy the last couple of games.

Bash shrugs it off. "Long as we keep winning, right?" he says and heads up Central Park West toward his building.

This week's folder is bulky. When it comes to this Saturday's opponent, Greenwich Middle, we can't just worry about a single player or two; we've got to worry about the whole team. These guys are like the Yankees of the Manhattan Middle School 3-A League.

Their scariest player by far is a midfielder named "Bull" Pike. According to the brief, Bull has been a football star since his peewee days, but when he got a concussion last year, his parents made him quit and take up soccer instead. Looking at the pictures of this maniac trampling kids half his size, I can see how he got his nickname. I can't help but wonder why his parents care so much about their son avoiding concussions but not about how many he seems to give to other kids. Not surprisingly, Bull leads the league in yellow cards.

Surprisingly, this guy hasn't gotten a red card since the first game of the season. After that one, his parents complained to the league people that it's not Bull's fault that he's so much bigger, and blah blah blah. Most kids know at least one kid with parents like that.

ON THURSDAY MISS Martina gathers us for another "absolutely exquisite" announcement. She's been crying her happy tears . . . again. Now what? Has some other anonymous person donated sequin spandex outfits to the class?

It's worse.

Miss Martina says that her application to participate in a citywide Viennese Waltz performance at Radio City Music Hall has been accepted. Maybe I'm a little distracted today with thoughts of Bull Pike turning me into roadkill on Saturday, but I'm not getting it. Miss Martina is gonna dance at Radio City? That's nice for her and all, but what's it got to do with us?

My partner Laverne Sneedly figures it out before I do. She starts bouncing up and down like she's on a pogo stick, clapping her hands, and saying "OMG" over and over again.

Then it hits me. Miss Martina isn't the one who's gonna dance. . . . *We* are. And the Viennese Waltz, you know what they call it in German?

Wiener Walzer

In only four short weeks, I'll be dancing the Wiener Walzer at Radio City Music Hall in front of thousands of people.

That night, I spend an hour researching whether I need my parent's permission to emigrate to Greenland.

SATURDAY'S HERE, AND it's a dark-cloud kind of day. Plus, it's October now, so it's chilly. It must've rained overnight, because the fields in Central Park are all soggy, and it looks like it could start pouring again at any time.

It is Columbus Day weekend, and we're a little shorthanded. A couple of guys are out of town with their families, and Coach Hornbuckle is steamed. While we warm up, he's tromping up and down our lines, pounding his fist into his palm, and barking away. Whole sentences aren't coming out, just words and phrases like "commitment," "brothers in arms," and "spree decor" (though I'm pretty sure that's French and I'm spelling it wrong). He's stomping so hard between our stretching lines that we get covered in mud, and we're looking pretty raggedy before the game even starts.

It's five minutes before kickoff, and Greenwich hasn't shown up. For a second, I think we might get a forfeit. Then, suddenly, from the far end of the North Meadow comes a caravan of bright-blue golf carts. It's the Greenwich Middle Dragons, arriving in some kind of motorcade. It's illegal to drive things like that around Central Park, but out in front of their caravan is a park ranger on a four-wheeler, which I guess means they've got permission. As they get closer, I see that behind the lead golf cart, they've got a little trailer crammed with dozens of trophies and cups.

"Do they always do this?" I ask Nick, who's standing beside me.

Nick says he's never seen it before, since it's his first year in the 8th-grade league, but that he's heard from some older guys about these clowns and their big entrances.

Coach is doing his best to keep us focused, but we're all just kind of staring. Their uniforms are bright, royal blue, and the players are all jacked. They don't look like a middle school team; they look like Chelsea.

Each of the seven golf carts is driven by a coach wearing a headset, and each is carrying three players . . . except for the last one. There's only one person in that one, and I'm not sure how he managed to squeeze himself in there. It's Bull Pike, of course, whose shoulders are wider than most school buses—let alone golf carts—and whose right leg is the size of a nuclear submarine.

Just then, it begins to rain.

I'd like to tell you more about this game, but I don't remember a whole lot, other than being tossed around like pizza dough and spending more time on my face than on my feet. We lose 9-nil.

That night, I dream I'm at the running of the bulls . . . and I'm not the bull.

Game	Result	My Goals	My Assists	Gallons of Central Park Mud Swallowed
JFK Ducks vs. Greenwich Dragons	L 0–9	0	0	22

MANHATTAN 8TH GRADE 3-A LEAGUE
WEEK 5 STANDINGS

Team	Wins	Losses	Ties	Goals For	Goals Against
Greenwich Dragons	5	0	0	32	5
JFK Ducks	3	1	1	17	16
West End Secondary FC	3	2	0	19	18
Washington Heights Rams	2	2	1	15	16
East Village Wizards	1	1	3	2	7
Harlem Aces	1	2	1	14	14
Soho Tigers	1	2	2	7	10
Battery Bruisers	1	3	1	2	4
CUAC	0	4	1	3	21

MOM SPENDS SUNDAY on the phone with
half the city, complaining about how rough
Greenwich Middle plays and how bad the refs
were. Based on the runaround they give her,
I can tell this isn't the first complaint like this
they've gotten. I tell her to forget it. If these
guys can get a police escort across the North
Meadow of Central Park, they've obviously got
more connections than we do.

Besides, we're still in second place, ahead of
West End Secondary School, and they're our next
opponent. If we can pull out a win against them, our

chances of breaking the JFK postseason drought are pretty good!

As for my Sunday, I should be reading *Tom Sawyer*, but the last time I tried that, I almost got eaten by my neighbors' Trashmas tree. I figure the Universe is trying to tell me something. . . .

I head down to the hair salon on the ground floor of our building, looking for Ronnie. I feel like I haven't seen him in forever, and I can't just call or text him. He's been on permanent weekend phone-grounding, ever since he got busted for turning Game Night at Sunset Terrace into a virtual-coin farm last year. Instead of Monopoly, Scrabble, and all the usual stuff, Ronnie introduced the retirees to the joys of mobile gaming. The old-timers got hooked, but they didn't care too much about all the gems, coins, and chests they were earning. They just liked playing the games. Go figure!

At one point, purple-haired Mertel asked Ronnie what she was supposed to do with all the diamonds and rubies she'd earned playing Major Miner. He explained that she could use them to buy things: better equipment for her miner, different outfits for her avatar, etc. She thought that was the dumbest thing she'd ever heard! Buying fake things with fake gems—pishposh!

Ronnie said if she didn't want them, he'd love to have them, since he was only seven rubies away from buying a halogen headlamp for his own miner. Mertel said sure and sent them over.

And from there . . . well, you can probably guess. In a matter a weeks, Ronnie was filthy rich in Major Miner gems, Assault and Tankery loot crates, Quilt-o-World buttons, and Siege of the Century gold sacks. So he started flipping the loot to kids at school for half the in-app purchase price. Genius!

The operation was humming right along until Frankie No-Shoes's granddaughter, Ella, had come to visit him a couple months later. When she found out her grandfather was a two-star general in Assault and Tankery, she was blown away! But when she asked why he was still bumping around in a starter tank, Frankie told her he didn't go in for all that new-fangled upgrading stuff and that he always gifted his loot crates to Ronnie.

Ella cornered Ronnie and tried to blackmail him into making her a partner.

When he refused, she ratted him out to the Sunset Terrace staff, who called his mom, and, well...

GAME OVER

Since then, Ronnie's mom has made him turn over his phone to her from Saturday morning to Sunday night.

So anyway, I go down to the hair salon, which his mom owns, but Ronnie's not there. I ask if he's at Sunset Terrace, and she says she doesn't think so. Then she gets this super-suspicious look in her eyes.

"Ronnie said he was helping *you* out today," she says.

Uh-oh. I'm in the my-friend-told-his-mom-he-was-doing-something-I'm-supposed-to-know-about-but-definitely-don't-but-I-don't-want-to-get-him-busted trap. I give her the old "Oh yeah, he is, I just forgot" line and try to get out of there without catching a shoe to the head. She's like a sniper with those things—I know from experience!

But she blocks the door. She says Ronnie has been helping me out *a lot* lately, and she wants to know what exactly he's doing.

Oh man. Somebody's gonna catch a shoe.

I tell her he's been watching one of the twins for me while I'm at soccer practice—which isn't a total lie, since he did actually do that—and manage to slip out the door before I cause any more problems for us.

I don't know where he is or what he's doing, but there's no doubt he's making a buck doing it!

AFTER PRACTICE ON Tuesday, Coach Hornbuckle hands Bash and me our Top Secret folders, just like he's done for the past few weeks. Unlike last week, though, this one is thin. It's all about one kid, and he hasn't even played a game in our league yet!

According to the file, West End Secondary School just got a new player—a Brazilian! His name is Carlos. Just Carlos. Apparently, he's so famous, he only needs one name. A bunch of Brazilian clubs are trying to sign him to their youth teams—the big ones, too: Palmeiras,

Flamengo, São Paulo. There are pictures of the kid talking on a cell phone, shaking hands with dudes in suits, hanging out with girls in bikinis. In every picture, the kid is wearing sunglasses.

Carlos's family moved to the US this week . . . just in time for West End's game against us. Perfect.

We spend the whole week at practice running isolation drills and working on traps. Coach even gives us homework: We've got to watch videos of famous Brazilians like Pelé, Ronaldo, and Neymar, in order to understand Brazilian *ginga*. It's their patented soccer style, and it's all about creativity with the ball, doing unexpected stuff but making it look like you planned it. Or something.

Wonder what my style is called? Do I even have a style? I've played pick-up games or just kicked the ball around Central Park with all kinds of people.

I don't know if all of that will help me on Saturday, but I know one thing: watching videos of all these one-name legends clowning world-class defenders and doing things with the ball that look like actual magic is giving me ulcers. This Carlos kid is gonna make us look like a bunch of bozos out there! And if we don't win, we'll drop to third place with only three games left. Just when things started looking up for the Ducks, we get steamrolled by a bull, and now we're gonna get pantsed by a Brazilian.

IT'S GAME DAY, and I feel like we've already lost. Yesterday, Coach Hornbuckle gave Bash and me a second Top Secret folder with additional information, er, "intel," on Carlos. The new file says that Carlos is *ambidextrous*. That means he can kick our butts with either foot. It also says that he might be a little late to the game because he and his agent (He's got an agent!) have a call with Real Madrid, which is also trying to sign him to their youth team.

Real. Freaking. Madrid.

It's a breezy, sunny day. Perfect fall weather,

actually. But to our team, it might as well be raining asteroids. That's how doomed we feel.

The game kicks off, and we realize that even without a one-named Brazilian god of *fútbol*, West End are pretty good. They're playing a tight game, focusing on shutting down our attack and counterpunching. Nick gets an early goal on a penalty kick, but they tie it up when their forwards break hard, corral a deep kick by their goalie, and one-two it past Brick.

So, we're hanging in there, despite the Brazilian cloud hanging over our heads. We make it to halftime tied 1-1, and still no Carlos. We're starting to think maybe he won't show after all. . . . And then, he shows.

We see the girls first. There are four of them. They are each over six feet tall and just unbelievably hot. Next, there's a guy in a suit and slicked-back hair talking on five cell phones at once. His agent, of course. And then, there's Carlos, strutting and smiling like a kid who just ate the last cookie in the box.

Just then, the second half kicks off. I don't even have to tell you that we're thrown off our game with Carlos's side show. I mean, how are we supposed to concentrate with all that?

West End goes up 2-1 on a crosser, and the first thing all of our guys do is look to see whether Carlos is coming in or not during the stoppage. He's not. Just doing some easy stretches—with his back to the field, no less! Like he can't even be bothered to watch our American version of *fútbol*.

Halfway through the second half, it's still 2–1. Coach Hornbuckle has stomped a 3-inch ditch into our sideline.

He's yelled his voice out, but he's still wheezing away and trying to get us to concentrate on the game, not the assassin who's preparing to come in and score 14 goals while his four supermodel girlfriends laugh at us.

West End's coach says something to the sideline ref who's in charge of signalling in substitutes.

Carlos takes his warm-up pants off.

We barely notice when West End thumps in a header. 3-1.

The ref whistles for subs. Coach Hornbuckle sends fresh legs in on defense, but we're all watching the other sideline.

Carlos does a hamstring stretch, gives a little grimace, tosses a "gimme a second" gesture to his coach, and starts doing some high-knees. He's not coming into the game yet, but somehow the fact that he's giving his coach orders is even more intimidating.

4-1, West End. I'm not even sure how that one happened.

There's another call for subs, but Carlos is on one of his agent's phones and gives his coach the universal hand signal for "zip it." He just shushed his coach! Coach Hornbuckle would call us names not even invented yet, make us sprint to New Jersey and back, and *then* kick us off the team!

5-1, West End.

Suddenly, we all seem to realize that there

are only a few minutes left in the game, and we are in serious trouble. We manage a couple good shots, but they've dropped everybody back into defensive mode, and the game ends 5–2, West End.

Coach Hornbuckle is so disgusted, he doesn't even have the energy for his regular postgame chew out.

He just looks us up and down and says:

"You durngum turd spankers just got butt-whupped by a lilly pickler who didn't never put a dadblasted boot on the dangbum pitch!"

Translation: We just got beat by a kid who never even stepped foot on the field.

Game	Result	My Goals	My Assists	Number of Our Guys Who Understand What Just Happened
JFK Ducks vs. West End Secondary FC	L 2–5	0	1	0

MANHATTAN 8TH GRADE 3-A LEAGUE
WEEK 6 STANDINGS

Team	Wins	Losses	Ties	Goals For	Goals Against
Greenwich Dragons	6	0	0	38	9
West End Secondary FC	4	2	0	24	20
JFK Ducks	3	2	1	19	21
Soho Tigers	2	2	2	11	11
East Village Wizards	1	1	4	3	8
Battery Bruisers	2	3	1	3	4
Washington Heights Rams	2	3	1	15	17
Harlem Aces	1	3	2	19	21
CUAC	0	5	1	4	25

ON SUNDAY, I'M looking for another sign from the Universe not to read *Tom Sawyer,* when Ronnie shows up at the door. Yes, Universe, I hear you!

We head down Columbus toward Andy's pet shop. I want to show Ronnie my chameleon, or, technically, soon-to-be-mine.

Ronnie's surprised that I've left my ball at home, since it's almost always attached to my foot. I think dribbling up New York City sidewalks—dodging strollers, hot dog vendors, tourists, and pigeon poop—is some of the best ball-handling practice you can get. But today, I'm too bummed about the loss to West End and our grim playoff chances to think about soccer.

Ronnie's down, too. He says he's had a problem with a client and has had to close his business.

Ah-ha! He started another business! That explains why he's been MIA (I must be hanging around Coach Hornbuckle too much.) the last few weeks. When I ask him about it, he says he can't talk about it.

"It's Top Secret," he says.

I stop in my tracks, right in the middle of the crosswalk on 72nd street. A cab driver lays on his horn to remind me to get moving again. I do, but I'm feeling a little dazed.

Now, maybe you're way ahead of me and you've already figured it out. But me, I feel like I've just woken up in the Upside Down.

"Ronnie," I say, "are . . . are you . . . Iron E . . ."

I stop there, because when I say it out loud, I feel even dumber.

"Yah!" Ronnie says. "You didn't know? Iron E. I,

Ronnie. How'd you not figure that out?"

So, yeah. *Ronnie* is the mysterious spy ring that's been supplying all those intel briefs to Coach Hornbuckle. That day he came to practice to keep an eye on Zane for me, he overheard Coach yelling something about how "those Washington Heights tater pumpers weren't about to show us any mercy." Turns out, Ronnie has a cousin that plays for Wash Heights, so he knew all about that team and the Egg twins. After practice, he went up to Coach, gave him some inside scoop—and got five bucks for his trouble. And here's the crazy thing: *I actually watched all that go down!* I just never thought to ask Ronnie about it.

So that's how Iron E. Intelligence Services was born. Since that day, Ronnie's been playing secret agent, scouting other teams, doing research on their players, talking to their families in the stands during their games and practices—the works! I picture him in a trench coat with a fedora and sunglasses, but I know it was just everyday Ronnie, doing what he does.

When we get to Andy's shop, just before we go inside, I stop and say, "Hang on, so what happened? Why did Coach Hornbuckle fire you?"

"Blowback," Ronnie says.

Huh?

He explains that in the world of espionage (cuz he's apparently some kind of expert now), *blowback* is what they call it when the one side plants bad info and lets the other side find it on purpose. Apparently, West End found out about Iron E. and came up with the idea to feed him a bunch of junk. And that junk? Carlos.

Turns out, the guy's not even real! I mean, the *kid* is real, but his name is Dwayne, and he doesn't even play soccer. It was all a hoax! Just some misdirection to distract us and throw us off our game. And it worked like a charm.

In fact, they based the idea on a real Brazilian guy named Carlos Kaiser from the 1980s. He's called "the greatest soccer player *never* to have played soccer." All he did was hang out with big-time soccer stars and pretend like he was one of them. He even talked on a fake cell phone, because back then, only rich people had them, so he knew it would make him look important. He wore sunglasses all the time and had a sweet mullet—all the stuff he needed to look the part. He looked and acted so legit, he got signed (and paid!) by a bunch of pro teams—and he wasn't even any good!

Whenever it was time to hit the practice field and actually start training, boom! He'd suddenly pop a hammy or something. All fake injuries, of course, but he kept faking it and clubs kept buying it. He even became friends with sports writers and got them to write positive things about him. He did this for years (*years!*) and never got busted. It's true. You can look him up!

So, that's it. We totally got *Carlos Kaisered*. Ronnie's

promising career as a sports spy: up in smoke. Our team's chances of going from the Sucks to the Ducks: a whole lot slimmer.

All thanks to West End and some kid named Dwayne.

I swear, if we walk in this shop and Andy's sold my chameleon, I'm gonna throw myself in the piranha tank.

GOOD NEWS! ANDY has kept her promise not to sell my chameleon, so I'm not forced to turn myself into fish food.

Ronnie is impressed with my chameleon, like I knew he'd be. He loves Andy's shop, too. And since she's not very busy today, she gives Ronnie a full tour while I hang out with my *chamaeleo calyptratus*. I study him closely, hoping to figure out how he does his independent eye trick. After a while, I've got a headache, and one of my eyelids is twitching weirdly. I think I sprained my optic nerve.

I hear Andy running Ronnie through the exotic pet matcher survey she's designed.

"I need to get a cleaner *what*?????" Ronnie yells, and they both start laughing hysterically.

I find them huddled around the computer on the checkout counter. Andy is explaining that a cleaner wrasse is the most entrepreneurial exotic pet there is—and therefore perfect for Ronnie.

Cleaner wrasses are little fish that live in coral reefs. Bigger fish come by, open their mouths, and these cleaner wrasses actually swim into their mouths! Sounds like suicide, right? All those big fish have to do is close their mouths and—*gulp*—they've got an easy meal. But they don't do it. The cleaner wrasses are too smart. They've worked a deal with the big fish. In exchange for protecting them from predators, the cleaner wrasses eat all the parasites and dead tissue out of the big fishes' mouths. Pretty cool. I mean, gross, yeah, but cool.

And—get this—the cleaner wrasses even offer better service to their most important customers! Customer service, preferential treatment, and home food delivery at the bottom of the ocean . . . crazy!

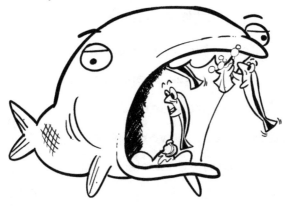

Andy is showing Ronnie videos of the underwater cleaning stations. These guys might be small, but they're smart as whips, know how to work a deal, and are brave enough to swim around in bigger fishes' mouths. Ronnie is in love.

NOW THAT RONNIE needs to raise a couple hundred bucks for a saltwater aquarium to house his cleaner wrasses, he's in full entrepreneur mode, which is good for me. I've managed to chip away at the chameleon fund, but I've still got a ways to go.

$140!

$125

$100

$75

$50

$25

Tuesday night, Ronnie shows up at my apartment for a strategy meeting, dragging a giant dry-erase board behind him. Most times, these meetings are just him brainstorming like crazy while I play video games and give him an occasional "Yeah, good one!" Once the dust settles, he's usually got a couple of brilliant ideas, and I can claim part ownership, since I helped, sort of.

I'm more involved than usual tonight, since I've got a chameleon waiting for me. Two hours later, we've got 22 schemes cooked up, but only two of them are rated Solid-Gold-Five-Star Can't-Miss Business Opportunities on the Ronnie Scale.

Solid–Gold–Five–Star–Can't–Miss Business Opportunity #1:
PET STORE MARKETING BLITZ.

The idea is to use Andy's brilliant exotic pet survey to match kids at school with their ideal pets. Once we've sold them on how perfect the pet is for them and how awesome the pet is to own, we'll tell them that we just happen to know where they can find that potbellied pig, striped ferret, or tarantula. (Not sure I want to meet the kid who matches up to a tarantula, though.)

We'll send them to Andy's shop. In return, if the kid and his parents say the survey is the thing that brought them there, Ronnie and I will get a kickback from Andy's dad. I think that means a percentage of the sale, but *kickback* is way cooler to say. Sounds like we're in the mafia.

Of course, we have to sell this idea to Andy, who will have to sell it to her dad, but it seems like a killer plan to us.

Capital Required (Ronnie says this is how much we'll have to spend on printing and other stuff): Medium.

Profit Potential: Medium.

Risk of Getting Busted: Low.

Consequences of Getting Busted: None . . . that we can think of, anyway.

Solid-Gold-Five-Star-Can't-Miss Business Opportunity #2: HALLOWEEN MAKEUP POP-UP SALON.

Ronnie's mom owns the salon on the ground floor of our building, remember? Lots of makeup and fake hair and other stuff down there. Kids need makeup and fake hair for their Halloween costumes. You see where I'm going with this?

Here's the plan: Ronnie's mom always throws a big party on Halloween, so the salon will be closed that day. We'll sneak clients into the salon in the morning and apply some pro-level cosmetic effects. We're talking blood and guts, hair dye and green skin, pirate beards and witch warts—the works.

I'm a little worried about how we're gonna actually create all those effects, but Ronnie says there are tons of videos online that'll walk us through it.

Capital Required: Low.

Profit Potential: High.

Risk of Getting Busted: Low.

Consequences of Getting Busted: Instant Death by Shoe.

Sounds great, yeah, but it's a little scary, too. The first time Ronnie set up a little side-business in his mom's salon, it didn't end well. A couple years ago, he started an after-hours pet grooming service. The setup was great. He'd get kids to bring their dogs or cats to the salon at night, and he'd do all the usual washing and drying stuff. I wanted in, so I convinced Ronnie to let me run a pet potty-training service. He agreed, but the test run went so bad, he fired me on my first day.

Other than that, the scheme was working perfectly, but Ronnie always has to add a special touch. He decided to start applying makeup. Fake eyelashes, weaves, lipstick, you name it. The kids loved it. The pets mostly didn't mind. And he was killing it profit-wise. But then, one night, he double-booked. A kid showed up with a pair of fancy Persian cats, just as he was applying his finishing touches to a Rottweiler named Bugler.

Those of us living in apartments above the salon thought World War III had suddenly started downstairs. The whole building emptied out to find Bugler, in bright red lipstick, tearing apart the salon, trying to eat Muffins and Marmalade (the cats).

Bugler, Muffins, and Marmalade made it out of there alive somehow. Ronnie . . . not so much.

I remind Ronnie of this and tell him maybe we should skip the pop-up Halloween makeup shop, but he's sure that we can pull it off. After all, it's only one morning. And it's kids, not animals. What could go wrong?

WITH IRON E. out of commission, there are no intel reports from Coach this week. I, for one, don't need it. We're playing Citiwide Unaffiliated Athletes Club, or "CUAC" (read: "quack"), and that means Howard Markowitz.

You know how in the Olympics, there's always that group of athletes who, for all kinds of reasons, don't have a country team to play for? So they march in the ceremonies under a flag with the five Olympic rings? The Cuackers are kind of like that. It's a team made up of kids who are homeschooled or go to small Montessori-type schools. Since they don't have a school team to play for, they get together and make their own squad. They usually stink, which is good, because we need a win . . . *bad*. Still, there's one kid on that team who I do have to worry about.

Howard Markowitz doesn't have good ball-handling skills. He's not very fast or big. He can't bend it, and he's not much of a defender. But he is one of the scariest kids in town, because instead of a right leg, he has a cannon. Which is how he got his nickname: The Howitzer.

I've been playing against this kid for years, and my mom got to be friends with his mom, which got me invited to his birthday party last summer. He lives in one of those cool high-rise buildings that has a pool on the roof. On the morning of the party, I'd been unable to find my swim trunks anywhere. That's when Mom walked into my room and handed me a red slingshot. I was thinking, "Sweet! That thing will launch water balloons for miles," but then she explained that it was my new bathing suit. Suit? That thing was barely a *bowtie*!

That's when Mom's Jedi-like ability to get me to do things I don't want to do kicked in. Here's how it usually goes:

So there I was, arriving at the pool party and hoping no one would think it was weird that I had a towel wrapped around my waist. Fortunately, we went early, so Mom could help Mrs. Markowitz set up. I jumped in the pool right away, thinking that if I was the first in and last out, no one would ever get too good a look at what I was sporting.

Unfortunately—and you knew there had to be an *unfortunately* coming—Howard had gotten a snorkeling kit for his birthday. Halfway through the party, he broke that stuff out, which gave him or anyone who took it for a test swim a perfect view of what was happening beneath the water's surface. I spent the rest of the party swimming away from whoever was wearing that mask, like a baby seal with a great white shark closing in.

But it didn't do much good. Word got out, and by the end of the party, every kid there had gotten a good look at my red slingshot. I could actually hear the chuckling sounds coming up from the snorkel. Maybe the most painful party I've ever attended. Thanks, Mom.

Anyway, the Howitzer is coming on Saturday, and with him a different kind of pain. Not emotionally scarring Speedo embarrassment. More like bone-crushing physical pain from a soccer ball traveling 8,000 miles per second.

Howard may not be that good or care too much about playing defense, scoring, or even winning. But as soon as his team is awarded a free kick, you can bet he's gonna be the one taking it. And the poor schmuck who gets between him and the goal is in for a world of hurt.

GAME DAY AGAIN, and it's the Ducks versus the Cuacks. Ha! Before the game, I give the team the lowdown on Howard "The Howitzer" Markowitz.

"Whatever you do," I tell them, "don't give these guys a free kick within twenty yards of our goal. That kid will send one of us into orbit."

If you're wondering what kind of ingenious plan I've come up with to defeat The Howitzer and lead the Ducks to glory, you're in for a bad surprise. I got nothing.

Fortunately, when the game kicks off, we are clearly the better team. Howard talks trash the whole time, like he always does. For this game, he has better material than usual, thanks to the Speedo incident. Whatever. Some kids talk smack; some kids don't. Like Coach Hornbuckle says, "Full battle rattle." I don't actually know what he means by that, but it sounds like it might apply to trash-talking.

Anyway, near the end of the first half, when we are up 4–1 and cruising, the worst happens: Calvin gets crossed up by one of their forwards and just grabs the kid's jersey as he's going by. FWEET! Free kick. Here comes The Howitzer, giggling like a kid at an arcade with 20 bucks' worth of tokens in his pocket.

As you know, I'm the shortest kid on the team by at least twelve feet. So what in the world am I doing on the wall, right? When you play for Coach Hornbuckle, you don't get to ask those questions. You're merely encouraged to "embrace the suck." I think that means we're supposed to just accept the worst stuff ever and get on with it, which may be good advice for life and all, but not when you're facing the possibility of getting decapitated.

So, here I am on the wall.

Now if you were lining up for a free kick and you saw this, where would you aim?

Exactly.

I remember Howard approaching the ball. Then I remember opening my eyes to see my mom, Coach, the ref, and my teammates standing over me. Mom looks scared. Coach looks, well, like he always does. The ref looks relieved . . . that I'm not dead, I guess. My teammates' eyes are big. Jungo, who hates the sight of blood, faints.

I SPEND THE night in the hospital. Everyone's worried that I have a concussion. I'm more worried about the fact that my face is so swollen I can barely see. The next morning, I look in the mirror. I look like I got punched in both eyes by beehives. I look like a caveman wearing eyeshadow. I look like somebody has surgically attached a giant plum to the middle of my face.

In case you're wondering, The Howitzer failed to score on his free kick. Thanks to my nose.

Mom comes in with a box of donuts. Like, real donuts—full of gluten, sugar, butter, and not

much else—which tells me right there how worried
she is.

"You won, honey!" she says. "How do you feel?"

If this is what winning feels like, I might have to
start throwing games.

Game	Result	My Goals	My Assists	Years until I'll Be Able to Smell Anything Again
JFK Ducks vs. CUAC	W 6–2	1	2	39

MANHATTAN 8TH GRADE 3-A LEAGUE
WEEK 7 STANDINGS

Team	Wins	Losses	Ties	Goals For	Goals Against
Greenwich Middle Dragons	7	0	0	43	10
West End Secondary FC	5	2	0	27	21
JFK Ducks	4	2	1	25	23
Washington Heights Rams	3	3	1	20	20
Harlem Aces	2	3	2	21	22
Soho Tigers	2	3	2	14	16
Battery Bruisers	2	4	1	4	6
East Village Wizards	1	3	4	5	16
CUAC	0	6	1	6	31

I SPEND MOST of Sunday on the couch with ice packs on my face. I'm hoping, praying that the swelling will go down. Otherwise, the kids at school are gonna think I've worn my Halloween costume to school a week early. I'm also hoping to get some good news about when I can play again. I don't have a concussion, but the doctor who treated me says my nose can't take any more rough stuff for a couple of weeks, at least.

That won't work. There's only one more week in the season—two if we make the championship game. Mom's been on the phone with doctors, fitness trainers, and who knows who else almost nonstop since we got home. I'm hoping she can work some of her phone voodoo and get me back on the field.

Late in the afternoon, I'm tired of lying on the couch. I need some peace-of-mind, but I don't want to go out on the street looking like a train hit my face. It's times like these when my fire escape comes in handy. It's the most relaxing place I know.

But today, I'm out of luck. Directly across the street, Mrs. Cunningham is out feeding the pigeons on her own fire escape. Most days, she wears her nightgown and wig when she goes out there. But every once in a while, well, she doesn't. Today is one of those once in a whiles.

Yikes. Plus, there's still a hungry Trashmas Tree just below, and to make matters worse, the guy who lives down on the third floor is smoking one of his monster cigars. I can't smell anything, of course, but that reek is so strong, I can actually taste it!

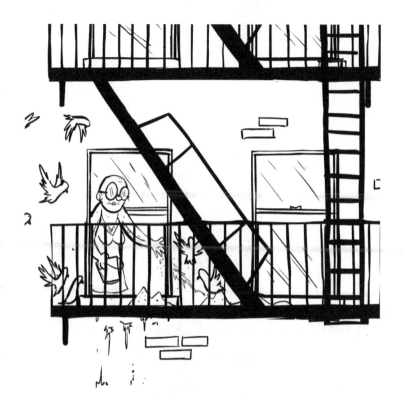

I give up and retreat to my room to start watching videos on how to create monster effects using salon supplies.

You might be wondering why I don't use this downtime to finally knock out *Tom Sawyer* and get the book report done. But that's the silver lining of this cloud! Looking like I do, there's no way Mr. Biesanz won't give me another extension on it. *Embrace the suck!*

ON OUR WALK to school on Monday, Ronnie
seems a little worried that my appearance will
scare off potential pet-survey takers. He's glad
I'm okay and all, but today is the day we launch our
pet-store marketing campaign.

Andy's dad has agreed to pay us a 7%
commission on any sales generated by our efforts,
but he refuses to use the word *kickback*, which
is a bummer. Seven percent sounds like peanuts,
but exotic pets aren't cheap, and Ronnie says
it's the best deal he could get. I was happy to let
him handle negotiations, but I did insist on one

stipulation (that's Ronnie-speak for "rule"): I want Andy to redo the survey so that there's no way a kid would ever be matched with a chameleon. Can you imagine if I raised all this money to buy him, only for him to get sold to some other kid? I think Mr. Biesanz would call that *irony*. I also think that Mr. Biesanz would faint from shock if he knew that I knew that.

As soon as the school is in sight, I get anxious. I'm sure my face is gonna turn me into an instant sideshow as soon as I walk in the building, and knowing Ronnie, he'll start selling tickets.

To Ronnie's surprise—and mine—my giant-plum nose and black eyes don't scare kids away at all. In fact, they have the opposite effect! Suddenly, I'm the main attraction, and not in a freakshow kind of way. Seems like the whole school has heard about the kid who looks like he uses a sledgehammer for a toothpick, and they want the story.

At first, I'm happy just telling them the truth, that my face got in the way of a free kick. Some kids laugh, some kids say, "Nice one," and some even say,

"Go, Ducks!" The whole time, I'm doing my best to hand out exotic pet surveys.

During third period, Ronnie texts me that we need to get strategic with this. He sends me some suggestions. They sound ridiculous, but when it comes to stuff like this, Ronnie's usually on the money, so I do what he says.

At lunch, with a big crowd around me, I tell a story about how I was in this crazy pet store with giant insects, man-eating snakes, and even a huge black bird that flies around like she owns the place, when—BAM—a rare tropical lizard called a Redwing Demonvenom bit me on the nose.

As the day goes on, the story takes on a life of its own. After school, Ronnie tells me that he overheard a girl in his history class talking about some kid in a pet shop getting eaten alive by a dragon.

Ronnie wants to go by the pet shop after school, so that we can report to Andy and her dad, but Artie catches up to us and tells me to report to the practice field. Because of my nose, I'm excused from practice, so I'm not sure what to expect as I head that way. Ronnie waits out of sight. He and his former client aren't exactly on good terms since the "blowback" incident.

When I get to the field, Coach has all the guys lined up in formation. That's normal—for us, anyway—except that the guys aren't stretching or warming up. They're just standing there. Coach is marching back and forth with Artie right behind him.

Artie has really gotten into this whole assistant coach thing, by the way. He barely plays at all anymore. Instead, he follows Coach around, keeps stats, takes notes, and does something incredibly helpful: he serves as Coach's interpreter. I don't know how, but Artie has cracked Coach's Oohrah-speak. Now, whenever Coach drops a one-liner from his military days on us (like, "Improvise, Adapt, and Overcome, lugheads!" or "Good Initiative, Bad Judgment, crumb bellies!"), Artie is right there to make sense of it.

Artie is lieutenant now, I think, but it's hard to keep up with all of the promotions and demotions. Artie has been telling us to call him "Lieutenant Artie" or "LT" for short. We messed it up and started calling him "LTRT," which sounds way more like the name of a droid than whatever cool-sounding nickname Artie was hoping for. So, naturally, it stuck.

Anyway, when I see all the guys lined up, I automatically head toward my spot in the formation. Coach stops me and signals for me to come stand with him and Artie at the front.

He barks: "BLOOD. SWEAT. AND NO TEARS."

He turns to me, hands me a little box, gives me a salute, and promotes me to sergeant.

Then he says the team has exactly 120 seconds of downtime before practice and jogs to the center of the field to wait for them. The guys surround me, pat me on the back, fist bump me, or muss my hair for the next two minutes. I feel like a cross between everybody's little brother and a favorite pet—but, considering how the season started, I can't complain.

They all head over to start practice, and I'm left standing there, wondering what just happened. Artie points to the box and tells me that it's a medal, a Purple Heart. They give them to soldiers who get hurt on the battlefield or, in my case, block a soccer ball with their face. He claps me on the back and joins the guys at midfield.

I catch up with Ronnie, and we head over to Andy's shop on Columbus Avenue. Ronnie can't wait to give his report, but we can't get inside the pet shop. We can't even get near the front door. There's a line of kids around the block.

HARD TO BELIEVE it, but there's only one more game left this season. By JFK Middle School standards, we're having an amazing year. But the postseason isn't a full-on playoff. It's just a single, winner-take-all game between the top two teams. Since Greenwich Middle is undefeated, they've already clinched one of the two spots—and people act like they ought to just go ahead and give them the trophy.

Coach tries to keep us focused on the next game only, but all of us know that West End is ahead of us in the standings. They beat us earlier in the year—thanks to the Dwayne-Carlos Kaiser incident—so, if we end up with the same record as they do, they'll advance to the championship instead of us. In other words, we absolutely have to win this weekend, and we need somebody to beat West End.

As if that isn't enough to worry about, on Tuesday I find out that the Radio City Ballroom Dance Torture and Humiliation Event is scheduled for the same Saturday as the championship game. No way can I do both, so if we pull off a miracle and make it to the championship, I get to miss the Wiener Waltz. If we lose, the season is over . . . followed by mortal embarrassment the very next weekend.

Talk about high stakes!

HALLOWEEN WEEK IN middle school is weird.
Some teachers are big fans, so they decorate
their classrooms, have Halloween-themed lessons,
and wear jack-o'-lantern stockings or ties.

Other teachers think middle-school kids should
be past all that by now, so they pretty
much ignore it. Middle-school kids are
stuck somewhere in the . . .
well . . . in the *middle*. It's dumb.
Because I'd bet any amount of
money that, deep down, every
kid loves Halloween.

Take Douglas Martelli. Today, Mrs. Jeffrey, the history teacher, sent him on an errand to her supply room, which is jam-packed with junk. Old maps, dioramas made by kids who took her class 50 years ago, and a bunch of other stuff—all of it covered in dust and cobwebs. Something about Halloween week and all those webs must have really gotten to Douglas, because the next thing we know, he pops his head out of one of the ceiling panels, singing the Spider-Man theme.

Unfortunately for him, Mrs. Jeffrey is not one of those teachers who gets into the Halloween spirit.

As for Ronnie and me and our makeup scheme, Ronnie doesn't waste time trying to sell our services to the jocks or the too-cool kids. He heads straight for the theater crowd, the after-school chess club, the hard-core video gamers. He even uses me and my bashed-up face as an example. He tells kids that the whole "blocking a free kick with my face" story was made up, that the swollen purple, blue, and red pouches under my eyes and the giant, busted nose are nothing but makeup effects, a promotion for Saturday's one-day-only event. We've got nine signed up for our Saturday morning makeup service—at ten bucks a pop!—and it's only Wednesday. That's how good a game Ronnie talks.

The customers have lots of questions about what they want done, like:

Can we do lightsaber burns?

What about gangrene?

Do we have enough gold glitter paint for full-body work?

I have no idea how to do lightsaber burns with makeup, I don't even know what gangrene is, and I have zero desire to apply glitter paint to every inch of another kid's skin. Ronnie, on the other hand, is in the zone. He's the master of promising everything and not really promising anything—at the same time. He says the key is to just get the customer onto the lot.

"Lot?" I ask him.

"It's a sales thing," he says, which makes me wonder if, sometimes, even Ronnie doesn't know what Ronnie is selling.

MOM'S PHONE VOODOO hasn't turned up any solutions for getting me cleared to play this week. But on Thursday, I'm allowed to return to practice, as long as I sit out any drills that might result in any person, place, or thing getting near my face. Even for the drills I *can* do, Coach puts me in the back of the line, which makes me feel like I'm back to square one.

I must be doing a bad job of hiding how big of a drag all this is, because Coach pulls me aside and says, "You're still top shirt, Sergeant. Just gotta keep your grape away from potential IDF."

LTRT follows up with an interpretation.

"You haven't lost your spot or anything," Artie says. "We've just got to keep your nose away from any other bumps. Doctor's orders."

So "grape" means nose?

"Well, no," Artie says. "It actually means 'head,' but your nose does kind of resemble a grape. Like, a really huge purple one with—"

"Yeah, I get it, thanks."

After practice I come home and find that everything is normal, which is to say, everything is totally bananas.

Z^2 are in the hallway outside our apartment. They've got both their heads crammed into the dumbwaiter, which is a funny name for a weird thing in a lot of old New York City buildings. It's basically a mini elevator that people used to raise and lower things from one floor to the next. But it's not electrical. It's hand-operated, like, with a pulley. I stop to find out what exactly the twins are pulleying up, and it's none other than Knuckles, our cat.

In the living room, Mom's hanging upside down from an aerial yoga rig and looks likely to fall on her head at any second. When she hears me come in, she opens her eyes and gives me a big smile, which looks pretty creepy upside down. She tells me there's a surprise for me on my bed. Marla is at the kitchen counter working on some new experiment. Probably another attempt at curing her hiccups. Poor Marla. She's going on ten months straight of almost nonstop hiccups. Maybe that's just how it is with science geniuses. Maybe Einstein had 'em too!

On my bed is an Amazon box with Mom's name on it, which could be good, could be no good. Inside is something called a Rhino Shield AX-2 by a company called IronworX Athletics. Sounds good! Even sounds kind of awesome, right?

Wrong. It's a bandit mask, the kind that only

covers your eyes—except that this one is made out of super hard, shiny plastic. *Neon-pink* super-hard, shiny plastic.

Oh, you gotta be kidding.

Mom comes in, super happy. She says that she spent days calling around until she finally found a doctor who was "solution-oriented." The solution? A nose-guarding face shield for athletes with broken noses.

"Sorry about the color," she says. "That's all I could get on rush order."

The good news: I can play out the season.

The bad news: I'll be playing out the season as Zorro Barbie.

HAPPY HALLOWEEN! THIS year, I'll be wearing

three costumes:

> Special Effects Makeup Artist
>
> Zorro Barbie Soccer Forward
>
> Pirate

That last one is really just a bandana and an eye

patch. Kinda lame, but Halloween for Ronnie and

me isn't about wowing people with our costumes.

It's about not disappointing the kids in our class

who are expecting us to show up on Monday with

bags of full-size candy at half-price.

But first, we've got some makeup magic to

do! Solid-Gold-Five-Star-Can't-Miss Business Opportunity #2 turns out to be . . . how can I put this . . . a little too highly rated on the Ronnie Scale. A dozen kids show up at the salon for their appointments. They've all got very specific requests for very difficult-sounding effects.

"I want the left side of my body to be cyborg, the right side lizard, please."

"Make my hair look like there's a werewolf standing on my head. Oh, and make my face a full moon."

"Pixilate me, like I'm a video that's buffering."

By the time we're done, only one kid is happy— and only because he wanted to look like he had a broken nose, which meant we could use me as a model. The rest are so mad, they demand refunds, and to be honest, I don't blame them.

Ronnie gives in to save his business reputation. We end up with $5 apiece, and the salon is a total wreck. I've got a game, so I tell Ronnie sorry, I can't help clean up, and duck out. All that planning for basically nothing.

I sprint toward Central Park with five bucks and a bandit mask in my pocket, although I'm the one feeling robbed.

MY WHOLE FAMILY'S waiting for me at the West 100th Street entrance to Central Park. Mom keeps giving me the devil horns sign to say how cool I'm gonna look in my mask. What's so cool about bright pink, I'll never know. Z^2 are both dressed as Robin and devouring Halloween candy they've already looted from somewhere. (Knuckles is back home in his Batman outfit.) Marla has earbuds in and is listening to jungle sounds. This strategy—not her magic potions—has kept her from hiccupping for 18 hours and counting. She hasn't gone that long since last

Christmas! I can't help but wonder if it's just building up in there somewhere, ready to erupt.

We're playing the Battery Bruisers. They're near the bottom of the league in terms of record, but near the top in terms of goals allowed, thanks to their goalie, who's known by his teammates as "JB." As I'm watching him warm-up, I'm thinking it might stand for "Jitterbug." The kid isn't that big, but he is super-twitchy. Like, he can't stand still. His fingers are twitching, his shoulders are scrunching and un-scrunching, he's bouncing from one leg to the next, shaking them out. He's sniffing, chewing on his lip. I think even his ears are moving. If you didn't know better, you'd think he was plugged into an electrical socket.

And when the warm-up shots start coming, I understand why nobody can score on this guy. His reflexes are *insane*. Seems like he's already moving to make a save before the shot has left the kid's foot! He's the kind of guy who can play doubles ping-pong by himself.

As if that weren't enough to worry about, we're about to take the field in front of what seems like half the school. Our crowd sizes have gotten better since the beginning of the season, but not good enough for Coach Hornbuckle. Yesterday, he made an announcement over the loudspeaker between second and third periods. It sounded like the whole PA system was gonna explode. Kids were covering their ears, running for cover—anything they could do to get away from the nutso drill sergeant barking orders at them at max volume. I doubt anyone understood what he was saying, but as soon as he finished, LTRT came on to say, "Once again, that's tomorrow, 12:00 noon, on North Meadow Field 4. Your 8th grade Ducks will be taking on the Battery Bruisers. With a win, we have a chance to go to the Borough 3-A championship game for the first time since 1992."

And it worked! Not only did a bunch of kids show up, but some of them are holding up "Go, Ducks!" signs. The cheerleaders for the football team are here, and everybody wants to take selfies with us. (Coach Hornbuckle isn't having any of that.) Suddenly, it's cool to be a Ducks fan. If we lose, we'll probably go back to being the Sucks tomorrow, but for now, the team is loving it.

Except for one kid. Except for the kid who has to wear a pink Zorro mask.

ONCE THE GAME starts, the other team is in my ear about the mask. Usually, trash-talking doesn't affect me at all. Today, it does. But it doesn't throw me off my game—it fires me up. I've taken an artillery shell to the face for soccer. I'm wearing a pink plastic bandit mask for soccer. And these kids wanna *make fun of me for it*???

I catch fire. I'm Ronaldo chopping, v-pulling, stepping over—every touch is a good one. I'm breaking ankles left and right. I set up Nick, for a shot that hits the crossbar, and Bash, for a header that Jitterbug somehow anticipates. But we keep coming. Possession after possession, I'm making things happen. Near the end of the first half, I even pull my nastiest-ever Maradona, and midway through the second half, I bike one that goes wide by two inches, max. The landing hurts, but it must've looked pretty cool, because our crowd is going crazy.

But for all that, the score is nil-nil. Their team can't get the ball away from me, so they've barely attacked at all. Still, that Jitterbug is making miracle save after miracle save. Against any other goalie, we'd be up 5. He's that good.

After the bicycle kick sails wide, the ref stops

play while someone retrieves the ball. I'm on my back, catching my breath, when somebody offers me a hand up. It's Jitterbug. He hoists me up, gives me a quick nod and smile, then goes back to set up for the goal kick.

I say, "Thanks," but he doesn't respond. At first, I'm kinda mad. Why be nice, only to be a jerk? Then I notice two bits of red coming out of his ears.

Ear plugs. He didn't hear me! I look at the Bruisers' side of the field and notice that none of their players or fans are cheering. They're all just sitting there, being super quiet and not making any quick moves.

So JB doesn't like loud noises. Makes sense, as tightly wound as he is. . . .

No time to think about it now, here comes the ball again.

Alex and I get a nice little two-man attack going, and just before I hit the box, somebody clobbers me from behind. Two more steps and it would've been a penalty kick, just me and JB. But the ref calls for a free kick . . . at short range . . . with a wall in front . . . and Jitterbug in goal.

I might be the highest ranking guy on the team, according to Coach's system, but I'm still the only 7th grader and half the size of everyone, which means I don't take the free kicks. Nick and Bash are standing over the ball, and Nick calls me over.

"This is all you, Chance," he says.

"Bend that sucker in, dude," Bash says. "You're *en fuego* today."

At this range, my best hope is to get enough spin on it to hook it around the right side of the wall and into the left side of the net. Too close to try to go over the wall. But one thing about having a weird foot: you can get some funky spin on a soccer ball!

I line up and take a deep breath—through my mouth, since my nose still doesn't work very well. I notice that it's suddenly very quiet. Either everyone is holding their breath, or I'm back in the me-and-the-ball zone. I steal a quick glance at my family. Mom is sitting with her hands balled up in front of her mouth, Z^2 are passed out on the backend of a sugar crash, and Marla is gone. Mom gives me the devil's horns,

which means "you rock," "you can do it," and "crush it,"
all rolled up.

I make my run-up, stick my plant foot, and swing
my right foot through the lower outside half of
the ball.

Then, several things happen at once—and all of
it seems like slow motion to me.

As soon as I hit the ball, I look at Jitterbug, not
the ball. I know I've struck it well, and I'll know
based upon his reaction if he's read it correctly.
He's already moving to his right, which means he's
on it. But can he get there in time? Behind him,

through the net, I see Marla returning from the concession stand with a big tub of popcorn. At that moment, the battery on her phone must have died and, with it, the hiccup-killing jungle soundscape.

From Marla, there is a brief, high-pitched sound, like the engine of a jump jet whining, then suddenly being cut off. The violence of the mega-hiccup makes her whole body jump, which causes the popcorn to erupt into a huge mushroom cloud above her. With his full attention on the ball, Jitterbug can't have actually seen the disaster behind him. But he and every living creature in the Tri-State area hears that hiccup— earplugs or not. JB's eyes bulge out, his whole body convulses, and he goes

HiccUP!

down like one of those fainting sheep.

Ball in top-left corner. 1-0, Ducks.

Their coach goes berserk at first, but for one thing, there's no rule about keeping quiet during games. For another, Marla is sitting on the ground, covered in popcorn, and sobbing between hiccups. She clearly didn't do it on purpose.

I'm taking all this in when I get mobbed by my teammates and our sideline starts going crazy. It's all I can do to keep my nose safe.

The game ends like that, 1-nil.

The first thing I do, after the final whistle, is run to the concession stand, spend that five bucks in my pocket on the biggest tub of popcorn they've got, and run back to the stands where Marla is. The second thing I do is head to Field 3, where I watch West End lose to Soho.

We're going to the championship game.

Game	Result	My Goals	My Assists	Kids Who Are Going to Call Us the Sucks on Monday
JFK Ducks vs. Battery Bruisers	W 1-0	1	0	0

MANHATTAN 8TH GRADE 3-A LEAGUE
WEEK 8 STANDINGS

Team	Wins	Losses	Ties	Goals For	Goals Against
Greenwich Dragons	8	0	0	48	13
JFK Ducks	5	2	1	26	23
West End Secondary FC	5	3	0	29	24
Harlem Aces	3	3	2	27	24
Soho Tigers	3	3	2	17	18
Washington Heights Rams	3	4	1	23	25
Battery Bruisers	2	5	1	4	7
East Village Wizards	1	3	4	5	16
CUAC	0	7	1	8	37

36

IT'S BEEN A big day already, but it's still Halloween—and Ronnie and I have work to do. He's in his Jeff Bezos costume, like every year.

Me? Forget the pirate! I'm not taking this mask off ever! I'm the Hot-Pink Bandito!

Not sure who came up with that nickname during the postgame celebration. It's not quite as cool as El Niño or the Bison, but everybody else seemed to like it.

Ronnie and I hit our target spots early, and by 6:30, we've filled up four pillowcases with full-sizers. Normally we'd keep going, but after the costume makeup fiasco this morning and the extreme exercise this afternoon (for me: soccer; for Ronnie: cleaning the salon), we're both totally exhausted.

Since his mom's Halloween party is in full effect, we head up to my apartment and watch a *Simpsons'* "Treehouse of Horror" marathon until we fall asleep.

Probably my favorite Halloween ever.

CRAZY WHAT A difference a week—and a win—can make. Last Monday, I was a puffy-faced exotic pet sales rep. This Monday, I'm the Hot-Pink Bandito, rookie phenom of the resurgent JFK Middle School Ducks 8th Grade Team and seller of half-priced full-size candy bars! By Wednesday, Ronnie is selling official Hot-Pink Bandito masks at $8 a pop.

As for the puffiness, it's all gone down, and all that's left is a dark-blue streak that runs under both eyes and over the bridge of my nose. Mom says it's *totally metal*, and for once, I kind of agree with her.

Now that we've qualified for the championship, I'll have to miss the ballroom dance nightmare-a-thon, but that doesn't mean I get to miss PE. We're into our seventh week of this stuff, and Miss Martina has slowly gone from a nice, ballerina-type lady to a big, screaming, sobbing mess. (The tears are no longer happy tears.)

On Wednesday, I tell my partner Laverne that I'm gonna miss the ballroom dance tournament, or whatever it's called. She says that it's called a *recital*, and that I can't possibly miss it. She immediately complains to Miss Martina, who talks to our usual PE teacher Mrs. Hurts, who isn't happy about it.

Mrs. Hurts has spent the last seven weeks in the bleachers watching MMA highlights on her phone, looking like she doesn't care a bit about ballroom dance. But now, suddenly, she's in an uproar about it, and it becomes a whole thing. They call in Coach Hornbuckle. Artie pipes up to say he'll have no problem making both the game and the Radio City thing. Of course. Like he's gonna disappoint his partner, Samantha. In the end, I'm right back to where I started: dancing the Wiener Waltz with Laverne and the rest of Peak Embarrassment.

I haven't given up hope that I can get out of this thing. If we lose, I'll be too down to dance. Surely Mom will understand that. Worse comes to worst, I can fake an injury or blame my nose.

And if we win . . . well . . . can't think about that right now.

Surprisingly, Laverne and I have our dance moves down pat. Somehow, I can do things with my feet I'd never even heard of a few weeks ago: natural and reverse turns, closed and open changes, the fleckerl, the reverse fleckerl, contra check, forward change, left whisk, canter pivots . . . You name it, we do it (sort of). It's way harder than I thought it would be—especially the reverse fleckerl, which is this crazy little cross-foot pivot that always lands at least half the class on their butts. Laverne and I have gotten pretty good at it; we only fall every third or fourth time.

After PE everyday, it takes me about an hour to get "1-2-3, 2-2-3, 3-2-3, 4-2-3" out of my head. I think I dream in ¾ time now. But it's almost over. This time next week, we'll be back to permanently damaging kids' self-esteem through good old-fashioned dodgeball, the way PE should be.

THE HALLOWEEN COSTUME idea didn't pan out like I'd hoped, and the pet-store marketing thing is done. Andy says that business has been so good that her dad hasn't had time to figure out what Ronnie and I will get as a commission yet . . . but soon. Selling Halloween candy added a nice chunk to the chameleon fund, but as of now, I'm running low on ideas.

Then it hits me,

that running low can be a good thing—a *profitable* thing. Especially at JFK Middle, which seems to be running low on a very valuable commodity: toilet paper. According to a special announcement by Principal Sprag, if students have to use the bathroom, they need to ask for a roll of toilet paper from Assistant Principal Freehold at the front desk. Pretty ridiculous . . . and embarrassing.

If that wasn't bad enough, Principal Sprag and his toilet stormtroopers started limiting bathroom passes to five per week. Things are getting ugly; kids are getting desperate.

But you know who gets unlimited bathroom

passes? Kids with medical conditions, like, say, a big broken nose.

I start flipping those passes for $2 apiece. Ronnie says I could charge more and tries to teach me about supply and demand, but I don't feel right price-gouging on kids who need to . . . well . . . *go*.

I've got cash coming in again, and all of it is a good distraction from the upcoming Championship Game. Despite all the good vibes about the Ducks at school, I can't help but think about our last obliteration at the hands and feet of Bull Pike and friends.

Don't get me wrong. I'm not scared. I just wanna win so badly that it hurts, and I don't wanna lose so badly that it hurts, too.

Coach Hornbuckle seems to know we're all feeling the heat and gives a speech about anxiety and nerves after our final practice on Friday.

"Take all that, chuck it in the burn pit, men!" he barks.

He might mean get rid of it or he might mean use it as fuel. I'm going with option two, no matter what LTRT says.

GAME DAY. CHAMPIONSHIP Game Day. It's

cold and gusty outside. We're past all the sunny

fall days stuff and smack into pre-winter now.

We're the only game today, so all the other

soccer fields are empty. The guys are nervous. You

can tell.

You know who's the least nervous, though? You won't believe it. It's Coach Hornbuckle. You'd expect him to be a knotted up wad of muscle and tension, but ever since we won last week, he's been like a different guy. He calls us "men" now, not "turdnuggets," "gnatfarts," or "boots." It's like we've graduated or something. He's still coaching hard, but we don't feel like we're the worst bunch of slackers on the planet anymore. He also still uses our nicknames, but after all this time, they don't feel like insults anymore. They're part of us.

Before the game, he pulls each one of us aside and gives us a quiet pep talk.

When it's my turn, he drops a beauty of a Sun Tzu quote on me: "Victorious warriors win first and then go to war, while defeated warriors go to war first, then seek to win."

I steal a quick glance to make sure my mom isn't watching, then I give him my best impression of a salute and say, "*Semper fidelis.*"

He bolts upright, salutes me back, and as I'm jogging out to join the warm-up lines, I glance back. He's still saluting, and I think that maybe—just maybe—I catch a quiver under his moustache.

Greenwich pulls their usual routine of showing up five minutes before kickoff in a motorcade of golf carts. Once again, the death clouds come with them, but today, it's some kind of awful half-frozen stuff that weather guys like to call a "wintry mix."

It feels right. It's more epic this way. More *metal*, as Mom would say. And Ducks like the rain.

We've got a surprise of our own waiting for Greenwich. Principal Sprag got special permission to run the buses today, which means that practically the entire student body of JFK Middle is here—not to mention all the parents, friends, and other folks!

Greenwich isn't short of fans either, but I don't think they were expecting to see this:

It's quite a sight, but the minute we take our positions for kickoff, none of that stuff matters. Right before the ref blows his whistle, something catches my eye. Standing by herself near the corner of the field, huddled under a tree, is Andy. But she's not alone! She's got a chameleon on her shoulder—*my* chameleon! She gives me a shy kind of smile and a thumbs-up. The chameleon is looking at me with both eyes.

I feel a surge of adrenalin and then—FWEET!—game on!

We're off like we're shot out of cannons. Straight away, Alex gets it to Hugo on the wing, who fires a nice little pass to me up the middle. I shake their midfielder, split two defenders, then hit Bash, who hammers one toward the near post. Their goalie lays out and knocks it wide . . . but just barely.

We might not have scored, but we definitely let Greenwich know that we didn't come here to polish their cleats.

Things tighten up after that. They start playing a little more carefully, looking to counter-punch, once they've figured out what we're doing on offense.

A few minutes later, I get possession near midfield. Their mids shift over to protect the flanks, and the defenders start backpedaling so that nothing can get behind them. All of that creates a perfect funnel down the middle of the field for me!

I bolt forward. I've got thirty yards of green grass in front of me. I see our guys working up both sides, being careful to stay onsides. Just as I'm getting ready to heel it back to Nick, who I know is behind me, and break into the penalty area, I hear heavy footsteps. Foot-thunders would be more accurate. Then, I get hit from behind by a wrecking ball that is swinging from a crane that is mounted on a speeding train that has been launched from a bazooka.

As I fly through the air, I see stars and then the sky and then mud, as I land somewhere in New Jersey.

There's a whistle. I look up from the cold mud to see Bull Pike getting a yellow card, only his 496th of the season.

I check to make sure I haven't re-broken my nose. All good there. Every other bone in my body? Pulverized.

Everything hurts, but I can't let Greenwich see that. As Bash pulls me up, I whisper, "You better take this one. I need a sec."

Bash gives me a quick nod, and I bend over like I'm straightening my shin guard. I notice that I've got a cleat print the size of a kayak on my chest.

Coach Hornbuckle calls out the first part of a Sun Tzu quote:

"CONVINCE YOUR ENEMY THAT HE WILL GAIN VERY LITTLE BY ATTACKING YOU . . ."

". . . This will diminish his enthusiasm," I say to myself. I must have memorized more of these than I thought!

Bash's free kick ricochets off the wall and straight up into the air. There's a big knot of people preparing to jump for it. The mass of bodies goes up together, a big, grunting, sweating ball of swinging elbows and jersey-grabbing hands, but the ball rattles around between them and lands in the grass, where I'm waiting. I'm on it before they hit the ground, and before their goalie can even register where the ball is, it's past him in the back of the net. 1-nil, and our sideline goes nuts.

The quote "In the midst of chaos, there is also opportunity" pops into my head. I look at Coach. His eyes are intense, but something about his moustache tells me he's gotta be smiling under there. Is he beaming these Sun Tzu quotes into my head?

After a brief celebration, we're back at it. Greenwich switches tactics. They can't run the funnel-the-little-one-into-the-middle-and-steamroll-him defense anymore. For one thing, Bull is now on a yellow card. One more and he's ejected. And, besides, it didn't work out like they'd hoped anyway.

They go into full attack mode. Their back line is playing up, their midfielders are pushing it ahead hard, and their forwards are making run after run into the box. Brick and our back-line guys are holding up pretty well, but it's a hardcore onslaught, and by the time the whistle blows for halftime, we're down 2–1.

2–1 is a weird score. It's got all kinds of baggage, depending on how you got there. If you go up 2–nil, then give up a goal, you feel like the other team has the momentum, even though you're winning. If teams trade goals to get to 2-1, it just feels like you're in a boxing match, duking it out with the other guy.

But if you go up 1–nil, then give up two straight, you start to wonder if that one you scored might have been some kind of fluke. It's not a good feeling, and I think Coach senses it.

He squats down in front of us and speaks softly. He's still barking, but kind of quietly, somehow.

WORM-BUTTS...
ZIT-WARBLERS
CANKER CRANKERS
...

"You men might think I stopped calling you 'dud-kickers,' 'worm-butts,' and 'scat-wheelers' because you won that last game," he says. "That by making it to the championship game, you somehow transformed from 'zit warblers,' 'canker crankers,' and 'diaper munchers' into men. But, Gentlemen, that's a bunch of bravo sierra—"

"Bull, um, bull stuff," LTRT clarifies.

Coach continues: "You ceased to be monkey puss after the last game precisely because after the last game, you, yourselves, decided that you were no longer monkey puss. I could see it in your eyes. And now, what I see is a team of soldiers who are about to decide that they're a bunch of fart-wagons after all. But I tell you this, men: it's all up to you. It's up to you whether you are going to walk out of here like warriors or limp out of here like a bunch of rut pickers. I already know which way it's going to be. Do you?"

Oohrah.

THE SECOND HALF STARTS a little slower, since both teams are kind of waiting to see what adjustments the other has made. We absolutely cannot go down 3-1.

Of all people, it's our back-line guy Jungo who gets us started. He takes on one of their forwards, and the ball ricochets off the guy's hip and shoots out into the middle of the field. Bull tries a quick change of direction but loses his footing and goes down in a muddy heap. That leaves Nick with some room.

Bash and I head upfield, him out front for a header, me a little behind, sniffing for rebounds.

Nick flicks it out to Hugo on the wing and trails me into the box. Two of their defenders move in on me. I'm totally sandwiched.

I back out of it, just as Hugo sends a hard roller at me. I prep a big one-timer with my right foot, and just as the ball gets to me, I swing just behind it. The defense falls for it and collapses onto the shot that never comes. I've let the ball slip right between my legs to Nick, who bangs it home off the left post. It might be the sweetest goal I've ever been a part of—and I never even touched the ball!

Tie game. 2-2.

Things are getting down to the wire when
Greenwich earns a corner. The kick into the box is
a high looper. The guys in front of the goal jockey
for position. Bull messes up and jumps too early—
at least, that's what he makes it look like. When
he goes up, four of our guys go bouncing off him,
which leaves three of their guys unmarked. And
one of them heads it in.

Hugo, Bash, Zach, and Calvin drag themselves
out of the mud.

Bull shrugs his hippopotamus shoulders, says, "I
always mistime those," and jogs back to midfield.
I can't see his face, but I know for a fact that
he's smiling.

3-2, and there's hardly any time left. Greenwich is in full-on keep-away mode now, but one of their mids gets sloppy, and it trickles out to Alex at midfield. Their defense starts backpedaling hard, and I give it all I've got on a sprint right up the gut. Alex passes it to me, and the defense is caught off guard. It's perfect.

I hear Bull coming from behind. I don't need a Sun Tzu quote for this one. My plan is to let him get close, hit the brakes, and draw a foul. That will let us get set up for a last-ditch free kick with our goalie in the box to help.

Bull makes it very easy—and very painful. Based on the distance I fly this time, it's obvious that his plan all along was to nuke me. Time is almost out. It's the last game of the season. What does he care if he draws another card?

There's a whistle, a card—a straight-up red, I think. But it could just be that my eyeballs are broken.

Our crowd goes nuts. Booing, yelling, the works. Even the Greenwich fans are wincing, like,

"Oh, yeah, that was actually horrible."

The ref blows his whistle again to end the game. Time is out, but we still get our free kick. I'm lying on the ground, blinking and waiting for all the pretty colors to go away. Finally, I get up and hobble into position.

Greenwich is down to 10 guys, because of Bull getting sent off. Our goalie Brick comes trucking into the box from the other side of the field. From a numbers standpoint, we've got a slight edge, although I'm not sure I count for more than about a third of a person right now.

Nick lines up, looks at the goal, takes his run-up, and dinks the ball straight toward the wall. Alex deflects it back out to the right side, where Hugo is charging full-speed. He crosses it, and Bash goes up, but its too high for him. At the far post, it collides with Brick's giant head, and into the net.

3-3. End of regulation.

There's a celebration, but it's short and kind of businesslike. It's not over. All we did was force penalty kicks. Greenwich, on the other hand, looks totally defeated, which is a win in itself!

We regroup on our sideline, and most of us just kind of collapse from exhaustion. The ground is soaking wet and cold, but so are we, so it doesn't matter. Artie runs around with Gatorade, while Coach reads off five names:

"DUNGBEETLE!"

That's Nick. *Good*, I think. *He's our best penalty kicker. He'll get us started right.*

"TOE JAM!"

Zach. *Okay. Not great with his aim, but he's got a big leg.*

"DIRT CRANK!"

Alex. *Yes. He's a lefty and has a nasty natural bend.*

"PUKE CANNON!"

Bash. *Yep. He's steady and reliable. He won't get rattled near the end.*

"FRODINHO!"

". . . ummm . . ."

Greenwich lines up their guys, and it's time to get PKs started.

Stat-wise, the Greenwich goalie, whose name is Eddie, is the second-best in the league behind Jitterbug. I don't know why LTRT chooses this moment to inform us of that, but he does.

Eddie is a stocky dude with big hands and huge ups—and he's crazy flexible. I watched him warm up before the game, and he was doing full splits and high kicks above his head. I don't know what he's trained in, but I wouldn't want to spar with him. He's standing by the left post of the goal, doing some kind of slow-motion meditation routine. Brick is leaning on the other post, doing . . . something less impressive.

We're the away team, technically, so we shoot first. Nick walks up. He looks confident as he places the ball, and even more so when he hammers one in low and left. Their goalie guessed wrong and had made an impressive, but pointless, dive to the right.

One of Greenwich's strikers, a kid with tree trunks for legs and a shaved head, strolls up and drills one top-right without hesitation. No chance for Brick.

1-1 after the first round.

Zach absolutely crushes one that just barely

misses the crossbar by about 47 feet.

The next dragon is a smiley midfielder who stomped on my ankles at least 700 times during the game. He smiles, rips one to his left, and right into Brick's paw, which swats it away. The kid stops smiling.

1–1 after the second round.

Next up is Alex. As predicted, he gets a wicked lefty bend on it. The ball catches the inside of the right post. Not a rocket, but perfectly placed, and in.

Greenwich trots up a short, ripped kid who looks mad all the time. He's got a natural slice of his own, but it's too much. The ball sails wide-right.

2–1 JFK after the third round.

Bash is up. He takes three chop-steps, and hits one hard and low, but right up the middle. Luckily, their goalie guesses left, and he can only get a toe on the ball as he flies in the other direction. It's not enough to keep it out.

Greenwich sends up their shifty midfielder Ruiz. He's quick and mean as a snake. He doesn't look nervous at all—even though he and everyone else knows that if he misses, we win.

He doesn't miss. He punches one into the side net and scowls over at us, like we owe him an apology for something.

3–2 JFK after the fourth round.

Now it's me. If I make this, it's over right then and there. If I don't, they've got a shot to tie it with their last kick and force another shot from each team. But I don't want that. Our team doesn't want that. We want to end it right now.

I'm worn out, and I've been getting absolutely hammered for the past 60+ minutes—not to mention the two trips into orbit I've received, thanks to Bull. I'm pretty good on PKs, but I'm not sure that I've got enough strength left to get one in here. I'm trying to think of the right Sun Tzu quote, but all I can hear in my head is "1-2-3, 2-2-3, 3-2-3, 4-2-3 . . ." Of all times, in all places, my brain decides to start *Wiener Waltzing*?!?

The ref gives a quick little chirp from his whistle, as if to say, "Now or never, kid," and I'm moving forward, before I can think about anything else.

1-2-3, 2-2-3, 3-2-3, 4-2-3 . . .

I plant my right foot next to the ball, swing my left foot. The goalie anticipates correctly where my left foot is aiming and dives hard to my right. The shot would never have a chance, if I'd kicked it with my left foot. But I didn't. With a little hop and twirl, I dink it with my right heel and send it rolling lazily, painfully slowly, almost crawling across the muddy grass, into the back-left corner of the net.

Championship	Result	My Goals	My Assists	Dragons Slain
JFK Ducks vs. Greenwich Dragons	W 3-3 (4-2)	1	0	1

MANHATTAN 8TH GRADE 3-A LEAGUE
FINAL STANDINGS

Team	Wins	Losses	Ties	Goals For	Goals Against
JFK Ducks	6	2	1	29	26
Greenwich Dragons	8	1	0	51	16
West End Secondary FC	5	3	0	29	24
Harlem Aces	3	3	2	27	24
Soho Tigers	3	3	2	17	18
Washington Heights Rams	3	4	1	23	25
Battery Bruisers	2	5	1	4	7
East Village Wizards	1	3	4	5	16
CUAC	0	7	1	8	37

CONGRATULATIONS
TO THE
JFK MIDDLE SCHOOL DUCKS!

MANHATTAN 8TH GRADE 3-A LEAGUE CHAMPIONS!

41

THE CELEBRATION IS a real blast . . . for the
people on top of the pile. I'm not one of those
people. And judging by the weight of the pile, I'm
pretty sure all of our fans, the cheerleaders,
the band, and maybe the
New York Giants,
have joined in and
jumped on top.

Several centuries later, everybody peels off, and somebody pulls me up from the muddy field like the Swamp Thing. Zorro Barbie Swamp Thing.

We line up to shake hands with Greenwich, and it actually goes pretty well. Most of them are better sports than I expected them to be. When I got to Dull Pike, he gives me a friendly punch in the arm that feels like a railgun shot.

"You're one tough little dude," he says.

Gee . . . thanks?

The weather keeps getting worse, so the awards ceremony is pretty soggy and rushed. It's pretty clear that all the adult fans want to get somewhere warm and dry, and all the kid fans wanna dance on the field and take selfies with us Ducks.

Me? I just wanna huddle up on my fire escape for a while to take it all in—but that's not happening.

First the good news: I spot Andy. I can tell she's cold, but she's still here! I run over and check both her shoulders. No chameleon. She says that he got cold, so she put him in her overalls with a little hot water bottle. She unzips it and we peek inside. He lifts one eye up and—I swear—he winks at me!

I tell Andy thanks for coming, thanks for bringing him, and thanks for staying.

"You bet," she says. "Wanna come by tomorrow and pick him up?"

I stare at her like Brick staring at an algebra equation.

"Your sales commission," she says. "It's over two hundred bucks at this point. The last two weeks have been the biggest sales weeks we've had since we opened. So, you know, he's all yours now."

I'm cold, I'm wet, I'm tired, everything hurts, I'm wearing a stupid pink mask—and I think I'm about as happy as I could possibly be.

Now the not-so-good news: my mom wraps a towel around me and hugs me so hard I feel things popping. She tells me how proud she is of me, how metal I am, and all that. What's bad about that? Nothing. But next, she says, "Now, come on. You need to get in a taxi. You're going to be late."

"Where . . . Where am I going . . . ?" I say, but I see the hanging bag in her hand.

"Radio City, Honey! Hurry now! I brought your tux. We're going to run home and change, and we'll see you after the recital."

42

SOMEHOW, ARTIE AND I are in a cab to
Rockefeller Center. I protested, but it was
hopeless. Laverne's parents raised a stink about
me missing the show, which led to Mrs. Hurts
calling my mom and informing her that my entire
grade for the semester was based on this show. I'm
willing to flunk PE to get out of this. Mom doesn't
agree with that approach.

Artie is prepared. He's got a backpack full of
wet wipes, towels, essential oil sprays, deodorant—
everything he needs to get himself fixed up for
Samantha. He's willing to share, he says, and

hands me a lavender-scented washcloth. I look
down at myself and dab the washcloth twice on my
arm. It comes away brown and dripping. My arm
is totally unchanged, though maybe it smells like
lavender now.

We hustle up 6th Avenue and just as we're
about to go in the performers' entrance of Radio
City, Artie suddenly stops and turns around.

"I gotta ask," he says. "That PK . . . was that a—"

"Yeah," I say. "Reverse fleckerl."

SHOWTIME! IT'S THE one and only, first ever, and hopefully last ever, Famous Viennese Waltz Extravaganza, or in German:

Das Weltberühmte Wiener Walzer-Extravaganz

They've got an orchestra from Austria, dance groups from twelve schools, and one Zorro Barbie Swamp Thing. This oughta go well.

Miss Martina is absolutely manic. She checks in Artie and me without even noticing that I'm covered in mud, then hustles off in a flurry of sequins and perfume to yell or sob at someone.

Laverne notices, however, and she's not happy. She practically drop-kicks me into a bathroom, and tells me not to come out until I'm presentable. And, by the way, I've got exactly twenty-two minutes until we go on.

I spend the first ten just sitting on the toilet seat, hoping to wake up in my bed and realize this is all a bad dream. I spend the next ten changing from my uniform to my tux, using wads of paper towels to scrape at least the topsoil layer off my hands, neck, and face. The rest of me is hopeless and will be under clothes anyway.

Just as I'm about to step out—with Laverne working on the door with what sounds like a jackhammer—I realize I'm still wearing my mask. I take it off, slowly, in case it's the only thing still holding my face together, to reveal the only area of my body that is not covered in mud. So now, I'm a reverse Zorro. Quite a look.

The performance itself goes pretty well. Maybe I'm suddenly feeling like a great weight has been lifted, maybe I just have a concussion, but I'm really gliding out there. And all the people, the lights, everything just kinda fades out as I'm doing my thing. I suddenly understand why some people dance when they're really happy. I'm not saying I'll ever be one of those people, but for those five minutes or so that we're on stage, I kinda get it.

When the show is over, the old Miss Martina is back, complete with eye makeup running down her face. Nothing but happy tears.

She gives me a hug and says, "I'm so proud of you, Chance! You really nailed your reverse fleckerl."

Ha! You have no idea.

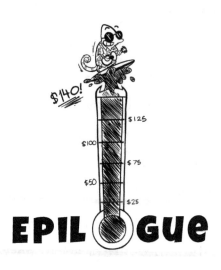

EPIL⬤GUE

THE NEXT DAY, Sunday, I go and pick up my chameleon, bring him home, and name him Elvis. Just seemed like the right thing to do.

Two days later, we have a ticker tape parade through the halls of our school, which gets a little out of hand when all the kids who've been carrying rolls of toilet paper in their backpacks break them out.

After that, there's a championship pep rally in the gym, and, that night, our end-of-season banquet in the upstairs room of a steakhouse.

Artie runs the show at the banquet, diving

into his clipboards full of game notes and stats and hands out awards. I win a lot of them. Like, an embarrassing number of them.

It's nice and all, but to be honest, that's not really my thing. All I think about the whole time is what Elvis is doing, and things like, *Is he hungry? And, I wonder if I can train him to walk on a leash?*

When all the awards are given out, desserts eaten, and congratulations shared, we take one more team picture, and everybody starts to head for the doors. A big paw grabs my shoulder and pulls me to the side. It's Coach Hornbuckle. He slaps a manila folder into my chest.

"Your orders, Sergeant Major!" he barks. (I got promoted again.)

His hand looks like it wants to salute, but he holds himself back and just gives me a quick nod instead. I swear his moustache is twitching again. Then he spins on a heel and marches away.

I open up the folder. It has a calendar of some kind, a list of names. . . .

"Orders?" I mumble.

"He means you made the all-star team," Artie says. No idea where he came from.

"Nick, Bash, and you," he says. "Well, don't look so surprised. You led the team in assists and were second in goals. Actually, you were second in the whole league in assists . . . you didn't know that?"

"No," I say. "Nick, Bash, me, and who else?"

"It's all there. Schedule, roster, everything. You start practicing in two weeks, I mean, unless you don't want to do it. But you have to. You guys have to represent Manhattan. You gotta show the other boroughs we can ball."

It's becoming slightly clearer as Artie walks away. The words on the calendar begin to take on meaning. Manhattan 8th 3-A vs. Brooklyn 8th 3-A. Long Island 8th 3-A vs. Bronx 8th 3-A. And so on. The names on the Manhattan all-star roster start to come into focus:

Craig Bakino

Greg Bakino

Sebastian Buchannon

Jimmy "JB" Buggs

Eduardo Capriani

Albert James

Howard Markowitz

Nick Neighbors

Bull Pike

Coach Hornbuckle is nowhere to be seen, but I feel a Sun Tzu quote bubble up from somewhere I didn't know existed: "Keep your friends close, your enemies even closer."

Welp, Sun, Mr. Tzu, whatever I'm supposed to call you, no problem there!

When I get home, I tuck Elvis in for the night and pick up *The Adventures of Tom Sawyer.* I read the same sentence six times, then put it down and turn out the light.

"Hey Elvis," I whisper. "What are the chances I'll be able to get another extension on the book report? "

Elvis doesn't answer, but I know what he's thinking: *One in a million.* I fall asleep to the sound of him munching happily on a fat cricket.

Acknowledgments
from Salwa Emerson

Thank you to Brian, my creative and stalwart co-author who has continually breathed new life into the book and has never stopped believing in Chance. Many thanks to Neil for your clever wit and talented hand—your drawings are legendary. Much gratitude to Teresa, our editor and designer, for your sharp eye, your diligence, and indescribable patience. Thank you to all my family and friends for rooting for this series—without your somersaults and cheers, I surely would have lost steam. A special thanks to all my crowdfunding supporters for your deep generosity and faith in this project. A very special thanks to my Kickstarter "super donors":

Claire de Perrot

Mary Abdullah (Mom)

Deepali Bagati

Lea Oglesby

Marsha Genwright

Mary Gallagher

Carissa Person

You guys are truly SUPER! Thank you to Stephen and Blake Spahn and the Dwight School for your decades-long belief in my talent and your avid interest in all of my endeavors.

ACKNOWLEDGMENTS
FROM BRIAN SALIBA

First, thank you to Salwa, my co-author, co-conspirator, and, at times, commiserator. Thank you for introducing me to Chance and inviting me to help build a world and story worthy of him. I hope that we have managed to do so and that this will be the first of many adventures we share with him. Thank you to Neil for bringing this first set of adventures to life in such an engaging, memorable, and perfectly pitched (kicked?) way. Thank you to my mom and dad. I'll never be able to fully express my appreciation for all you have done and continue to do—let alone repay it—but I'll keep trying! Thank you to my brothers, Craig and Brett, for showing me how to grow up and helping me remember not to. Thank you to Rosie for the endless love and support—and for absolutely never doubting any of this. And thank you to Winnie for always reminding me when it's time to take a break and go for a walk outside.